I've watched too many young girls experience this kind of trauma and the consequences. *Choices* is a book that will encourage deeper understanding and a dialogue about these very prevalent and disturbing teen issues.

Terry Steege
Women's health care nurse practitioner
Grandview Clinic, Ironwood, MI

After eighteen years as a school counselor, I know that teens are hungry for stories that reflect their lives. They want to see characters go through difficult times and come out the other side, changed but better. I highly recommend *Choices*. This book will empower readers and give them hope. An important read for teens everywhere!

H. E. Fleishman
MS, educational psychology
Los Angeles, CA

A riveting and noteworthy young adult novel to which all ages can relate. *Choices* explores sensitive topics in a compelling and engrossing story.

Kathy Costa
Youth Outreach Librarian
Santa Fe, NM

Teen readers review *Choices*:

Juno meets real life. This book is a great read, it's very real and down-to-earth. It's written very well and very emotional. I loved it!

Makena M., age 16
San Diego, CA

… it is the heart of this book that makes it such a wonderful read. Hard to put down!

Tatiana M., age 17
Gloucester, MA

I really enjoyed this book. We can all relate to something in this story!

Tabytha Joy, age 15
For *Reader Views*
Austin, TX

I loved *Choices*! The characters felt so real; I couldn't stop reading!

Alexandra D., age 16
Philadelphia, PA

Male or female, young or old, everyone can understand the emotional turmoil of this young girl's struggle.

Isaac G., age 16
Santa Fe, NM

Choices

A Novel

Kate Buckley

 Book Publishers Network

Book Publishers Network
P.O. Box 2256
Bothell • WA • 98041
PH • 425-483-3040
www.bookpublishersnetwork.com

Because of the dynamic nature of the Internet, any Web addresses or links contained in this book may have changed since publication and may no longer be valid.

This is a work of fiction. All of the characters, names, incidents, organizations, and dialogue in this novel are either the products of the author's imagination or are used fictitiously.

Printed in the United States of America
10 9 8 7 6 5 4 3 2 1

Library of Congress Control Number: 2009655030
LC Classification: PS3602.U26485 C56 2007
ISBN10: 1-935359-12-6
ISBN13: 978-1-935359-12-8

Editor: Julie Scandora

For Steve, Kyle, and Jackson,
with love and appreciation.
You are always in my heart.

Contents

Hey—What's Your Name?

I wanted to look just right. Lifting a few earrings out of my jewelry box, I held them up to myself in the mirror, one at a time. The peridot dangles were perfection with my lime-green sweater and black jeans.

Oh yeah, I was ready.

Mel, Dakota, Jenna, and I were going to Cherry Creek High's basketball game. It took several days, but Mom finally convinced my Dad that I'd be safe going out to a night basketball game. Jeez. She was all smart about it too, deemphasizing the coed environment factor and playing up the fun I'd have going to the game with my girlfriends from school. Just Innocent—with a capital *I*—fun.

Getting all A's on my report card didn't hurt either.

Still, with a father like mine, it might be a year before I'd get to go out at night again. I dabbed a little of my new lip gloss on and read the label: "Hot Stuff." I smoothed on some more and dusted my cheeks with blush.

I examined myself up close. My breath formed a circular pool of mist on the mirror's smooth surface. Grandma had given me the mirror for my fifth birthday and told me it was magic, like the one in *Snow White*. Though I could only see the top of my head at the time, I believed that the taller I grew and the more visible I became the more beautiful I'd be. Someday, I thought, I'll be the fairest of them all, just like Snow White. Roses and tiny clusters of leaves were carved into the mirror's wide, silvered frame. The mirror had been Grandma's from the time she was a young girl until my grandfather died, and then she'd given it to me. Of everything in my room, it was my most favorite.

The girl I was and the person I was becoming stared back. The fairest? Maybe not, but I was really OK with how I'd turned out. My toffee-colored hair was long and full. My round, wide-set eyes were the shape of Mom's. They were the blue-green color of my father's; I had his straight nose and high cheekbones, too.

People often said I should be a model, but I was way too shy for that. My mother told me I'd gotten the "best of both of them," but in my opinion, I was really more a combination of Grandma and my Aunt Sarah.

"Kara, Mel's here!" Mom called.

I grabbed my leather jacket from the bed and raced downstairs.

The parental gauntlet was lined up by the front door. I had to pass inspection just to get out of my own freaking house. Thank God there were only two of them. My father would typically say I had on too much makeup or tell me to change my sweater because it was "too small." All I ever got to do was go to church, school, or dumb sleepover parties.

Mel was standing beside my Dad. She winked at me when he gave me his usual, the worried once-over. His face was a mask of sadness. Mel's excuse for my father's weirdness was that he probably loved me too much, but I knew better. He never wanted me to look hot. God forbid I might be attractive to a boy. Why couldn't he just be proud of me or engage in some normal fatherly activity?

"Don't be late," he said, all serious.

"Fab earrings," Mel said.

I smiled at Mel and scooted by my father.

"You look great, sweetie. Got your cell phone?" Mom asked.

I nodded and patted my jacket pocket.

Mom touched my shoulder as I passed her. "Have a good time."

And Mel and I were out the door.

Free!

Dakota and Jenna had already been picked up. I climbed in back with them, and Mel sat up front with her mom.

What a pitiful foursome: Stuck in an all-girls school, none of us had boyfriends or driver's licenses. We were pathetic, no doubt. We laughed, talked, and squealed the whole way to the game. Our excitement filled the Subaru, gushing out of us like first-time nominees on their way to the Academy Awards. Or something bigger, something unimaginable.

I swear, I felt so alive, like my whole life was about to begin. I was really out, at night, with tons of other kids, a part of the real world. It was about time.

The front of Cherry Creek High was a swarm of kids. Luckily, we already had our tickets.

"I'll meet you by the entrance to the parking lot at nine thirty. Have fun!" Mel's mom called.

We burst out of the car a few minutes before game time.

The air in the overcrowded gym had a moist, sweaty smell. The bleachers were jammed, pulsing with noise and energy.

"This is so awesome!" I shouted to Mel. Mel nodded and pointed to a place in the second row on the Cherry Creek side. There were no open seats but, as usual, we all followed Mel anyway.

"Can't you guys squeeze in? Jeez!" Mel yelled as we climbed over some Cherry Creek girls. They grudgingly moved over, letting the four of us wedge ourselves into a space on the bleachers barely big enough for two.

The snotty Cherry Creek girls sneered, and Mel sneered back. Mel had the best sneer. She could make anyone feel like dirt in a flash.

The gym was sweltering hot. I took my jacket off, shoved it under me, and smiled to myself. Not only had I wrestled permission from my parents to go to a night game, now Mel had scored us great seats.

"JAKE, JAKE, JAKE!!!"

And then I saw him: Jake Dodson, charging down the court full speed, dribbling the ball so fast I could barely see it. All muscled and lean, Jake's thick hair moved up and down with his giant strides.

In a word—gorgeous.

He was totally amazing. Jake stopped short and hit a perfect shot before I could let out my breath. The crowd went wild.

"JAKE, JAKE, JAKE!!!"

The four of us screamed and clapped along with everyone else.

"Isn't he so awesome? His picture is in the paper *all* the time!" Dakota shouted over the excited crowd.

I never read the *Denver Post* or the *Rocky Mountain News* unless I had to cut out an article for current events in global studies class. No way did I ever read the sports page. But I would now.

Dakota knows everything about public school stuff. Her mother is a counselor at one of the middle schools, and her father is the assistant football coach at Cherry Creek. Even though this game had been sold out, Dakota's dad was able to get us tickets.

In between Jake's scoring about a million points and the crowd's screams, Dakota told us he was a senior and the captain of the basketball team. She said he was the coolest boy in the coolest crowd of any school in Denver. No doubt.

Cherry Creek slaughtered the other team, a total massacre. They won by sixty-three points, and Jake scored most of them.

The bleachers emptied.

Jenna, Dakota, and Mel went to wait in the long bathroom line while I hung out by the concession stand in a total happiness trance.

Kids shrieked and screamed at the Cherry Creek guys when they left their locker room. Girls and boys were pushing and shoving to get closer to the team; it was like they were celebrities. Boys high-fived Jake, and girls reached up to pat him on the back. Some nervy blond girl even touched the back of Jake's hair.

Jake's eyes grazed the room. Then he saw me, and his eyes kind of locked on me. Intense. I smiled and glanced over at the bathroom, a slight panic thumping my heart. Where was Mel? My friends?

I looked back to see Jake still smiling, big—right at me. He said something to the rest of the guys and started toward the concession stand. He was headed toward me. I glanced behind me and next to me. Jake had to be heading for someone else, not me. Maybe he wanted a Frito pie or a hot dog? Then Jake was there, standing right in front of me—all six feet, three inches of him.

"Hey. Like the game?"

"It was awesome. You were awesome!" Ugh. Why did I say that? I felt my face getting all hot.

"Thanks. Haven't seen you around. You go to Cherry Creek?"

"No."

"East High?"

"Saint Ursula's." Double ugh. Admitting that I went to Saint Ursula's Academy for Girls was sure to end the most incredible moment of my life before it even began.

"Cool. I hear that's a pretty good school. What's your name?"

"Kara."

"Mine's Jake."

Oh yeah it is. Like everybody didn't know; like he wasn't famous, a superstar.

Mel and Dakota walked out of the bathroom, blabbing away. Then Mel saw me. She stopped and grabbed Dakota's arm. They froze midstep—wide-eyed and drop-jawed. Jenna was last out. Mel pointed in my direction and pulled her over beside them. The three goggle-eyed girls stood there, gawking at Jake talking to me.

Thank God Jake had his back to them.

"There's a party after the game, at a friend's house. Want to go?"

Omigod. Me? *Me*? "Um, I can't."

Jake seemed blown away. No sane girl in Denver would say no to him. The only girl stupid enough to say no would be a pathetic girl from Saint Ursula's, a girl with a ten o'clock curfew.

"Oh. You here with someone?"

"Yeah, sort of," I muttered, unable to arrange two coherent thoughts.

Jake took a program from a pile on the concession stand and reached into his jacket pocket for a pen. "What's your last name, Ms. Kara? Give me your number, and I'll call you sometime."

My hand trembled, and my writing was pathetic scribble, but I wrote "Kara MacNeill" and my cell number on the program and handed it back.

"Cool. Thanks." Jake smiled. He nodded to me and walked off.

I had one single thought: He has the best smile on the planet.

Mel, Dakota, and Jenna ran over to me, their voices merging into one huge blurt of questions.

"Did he just, like, walk over to you?"

"Omigod, was that Jake? Jake Dodson?"

"What did he say?"

"Did he, like, ask you out?"

All I could manage to say was, "Yes." I was in a daze, staring at the floor where Jake had stood, like it was holy ground. My whole life had changed in a nanosecond.

"Oh, WOW. Really?"

"Omigod! He's so gorgeous, an absolute god!"

"Jenna, please. Let us not blaspheme." Mel's imitation of our homeroom teacher, Sister Elaine, was perfect. We all laughed.

My mind was a blur, afloat in an ultimate dream world instead of my usual boring reality. My friends were really excited for me, and maybe just a little jealous.

My feet kind of glided across the front lawn after Mel's mother dropped me off. I bounded through the entryway, down the hall, and into the den. All I could think about was Jake's face, his smile, his deep voice.

My parents had the television tuned to CNN. My mother was sitting on the edge of the beige sofa working on a needlepoint, her brow set in a squint of concentration. My father sipped his Scotch and made some notes on a legal pad he was balancing on his lap. He glanced at his watch. "You're late."

The ice tinkled, the amber liquid in his glass created a little cyclone as he swirled his drink and rested it carefully on the arm of his chair.

Mom looked up from her stitching and smiled. "Did you have fun?"

"Yeah, it was pretty great. Cherry Creek killed them."

My father tapped his finger on the face of his watch. "Your curfew was ten."

"Sorry, Dad. It's only ten minutes. We dropped Jenna off first."

"She knows, Bill," Mom said. "Next time she'll ask to be dropped off first, won't you, hon?"

Next time. If my mother weren't around, there wouldn't be one.

"Yeah, I will, promise."

My father sighed, took another sip of his Scotch, and returned to his paperwork.

Phew.

"OK, 'night," I called and took the stairs two at a time up to my room. I couldn't wait to get away from them so I could think about Jake in the quiet of my room. I wanted to remember every detail about him, our conversation, the way he'd zoomed into my eyes with his crystal blue ones.

I needed to figure out a way to see him again, to go out with him. The idea of actually going out with a guy seemed impossible. My parents could never know.

I closed my bedroom door and sat down at my desk, still floating. My phone rang, and I pulled it out of my pocket. I didn't recognize the number.

"Hello?"

"Hey, it's Jake Dodson. How's it going?"

"Um, fine." I sounded so lame!

"The party was a total bore. I left early, thinking about you. Wish you could have come along," he said.

"Yeah, um, sorry." I couldn't believe it was Jake, calling me. His voice was deep, as beautiful as his smile—and my replies were pitiful.

"There's gonna be a party after my game next Friday. Think you can make it?" he asked.

"Uh, what time…where will it be?" I had no idea how I would get out but…whatever it took.

"The usual. About ten or so. It'll be at Dell's. He's on the team." I twisted a piece of my hair around my finger until I'd cut off the circulation and thought of Jake's smile.

"I think so, but, um, can I, like … get back to you?"

Jake was silent for a second, probably thinking how pathetic I was, probably wishing he hadn't called and wondering why I couldn't just say "Yes" or "No" like a normal person. My mind raced. What cool thing could I say? How to not sound like a total, drooling bore?

"Sure, just call my cell and let me know. Call me anytime." Jake paused then said, "See you soon, Kara."

And he was gone.

"Bye," I said to a dead phone, my sweaty fingers still clutching it.

This was real. Jake was asking me out. He wanted to see me again, to take me to a cool party with all his cool friends.

Omigod. Omigod.

I was so jazzed I thought I might burst into a zillion pieces.

Out the Window

Rules, ludicrous rules—at school, at home, everywhere—strangling my life, squeezing it into a tiny box and clamping down on the lid.

A ten o'clock curfew for a fifteen-year-old was so lame.

One of the gazillion ridiculous rules my father had was no going out with guys until I turned seventeen. In two years my curfew would be ten-thirty. Whoopee. Nothing even started happening in Denver until after ten. Who was going to ask me out for a half-hour date? No one. Definitely not Jake.

My parents were in their bedroom with the door closed. The ten o'clock news droned out into the hallway from their TV. I grabbed an extra pillow from the linen closet and carried it back to my room, tiptoeing. Jake would be out in the alley behind my garage in a few minutes. I could hardly wait.

Jake had three hours of basketball practice every day, and then there was me, locked away on the opposite end of town at Saint Ursula's All-Girls Prison. At night, I was trapped in my own private jail: home. For Jake and me, getting together was almost impossible. Almost.

I laid three pillows lengthwise on my mattress and covered them with my comforter then smashed and pounded them into the shape of me, sound asleep. It looked pretty real, too. Maybe a long wig would make it even better. I made a mental note to search through my box of old Halloween costumes in the basement.

My control freak father was never going to change my curfew or let me go out at night. The only option was to sneak out my window, crawl across the roof, and then climb down the lattice to the driveway. This would be my second time, and I was already pretty good at it.

Jake was absolutely the most beautiful boy ever—in the movies, in magazines, anywhere. His hair was deep brown with hints of auburn when the light hit it; thick black lashes set off his ice-blue eyes perfectly. I loved the way his hair fell over one eye sometimes and the way he threw his head back when he laughed. If things kept going right with us, sneaking out could be a regular thing.

And Jake was so worth it.

Ultra wired and excited, I almost slipped and fell going down the dumb lattice. The ultimate bummer would be breaking a leg and getting grounded for the rest of high school. I sprinted across my backyard and down the alley behind my house.

Jake was standing in the shadows of the street lamp, warming his face with gloved hands. When he saw me, he broke into a huge grin.

"Hey. Am I late?"

"No. You're perfect," he said, beaming his killer smile at me.

Omigod. I smiled right back.

Jake opened the car door for me, and I slid in. He was wearing his red and white Cherry Creek jacket. "DODSON" blazed across the back of it in big white letters; underneath his name was his number, 21.

My whole body was tingly, on fire.

After we drove out of the alley and away from my neighborhood, I started to relax.

"Like Bob Marley?" Jake put a CD into the player.

"Oh yeah, he's awesome."

Jake cranked up the volume. "Soul Captive" blasted through
the car.

The cold winter air, the music, being with Jake, all of it felt magical.

"Ever been to a bonfire?" Jake asked.

"No."

I'd never been anywhere. *Anywhere.*

We drove to the other side of town. About twenty cars were parked
in a dirt lot next to a big, open field. Jake pulled in.

"I think you'll like this," he said, and leaned across my lap
to unlatch my door and push it open. The light above the dash
went on.

Jake's long body was touching my jeans, my legs. My heart
almost stopped. He pulled himself back into his seat and sat there,
his eyes fixed on me. The car light was shining on Jake's perfectly
straight white teeth and the thick, gorgeous hair that spilled over
his forehead. I wanted like crazy to touch it. His eyes stayed focused
on me.

"Is something wrong?" I asked.

In the surrounding blackness, sticks crunched under sneakers.
Kids were talking and laughing.

Jake stared deep into my eyes, a grin creeping across his face.
"Not a thing. It's just you. You're really pretty." Jake turned and
opened his own door, signaling to me with his hand. "Come on,
beauty. Let's go."

I floated out of his car, a lit match against the dark night sky.

Giant logs, scraps of lumber, and tree branches were heaped in
a pile on top of a mound of ash and charred wood in the middle of
the field. A few cases of beer and bottles of liquor were stacked near
one of the parked cars.

Jake walked over to a guy who was taking bags of ice out of the trunk of a car.

"Kara, this is Dell. Dell's on the team."

Dell turned from his ice bag duties and saluted me. I recognized him from the game. He was tall and huskier than Jake, not nearly as good looking.

"Hey there." He nodded to Jake and raised an eyebrow, like he approved of me.

"We're just about to light 'er up. There's a party at my house after. The 'rents are away."

"Cool," Jake said, he turned to me. "Sound good?"

It was a moonless night. I could barely see his face, and I hoped my nervousness didn't show. "Maybe," I said, afraid to stay out too late and push my luck, but much more afraid to admit it.

Jake popped the top of a can of beer and offered it to me.

"No. No, thanks."

"Don't like beer?" Dell asked. "We've got plenty of other treats. How about a melon cooler?" He reached for a six-pack.

"Thanks, I'm good."

A whoop exploded from the crowd as someone put a lit torch to the pile of wood. The roar from the fire was intense.

Loud. Crackling. Explosive.

"Kerosene does the trick," Jake said.

"Every time," Dell replied, and they clinked their beer bottles in a toast.

Jake took my hand and led me over to the crowd by the fire. I could see faces now. None of them were familiar, and all of them were older than mine.

A group of girls stood next to us. The same girls I'd seen crawling all over Jake by the locker room after his game.

Jake nodded to them and pointed at me.

"Kara, meet 'the girls'; girls, this is Kara."

Some mumbled "heys" drifted my way. Their eyes moved up and down, up and down. They exchanged glances, checking me out.

"Cheerleaders," Jake whispered into my ear and put an arm around me, pulling me close. My body grew hot, alive.

The fire roared. Sparks and burning ash flew high above us and disappeared into the clear, cold sky.

"Cool, huh? I love fires," Jake said.

"Me too."

We stood there, watching it burn, hypnotized by the flames.

Somebody passed a bottle of tequila around. I handed it to Jake when it came by. He took a long swig and passed it on.

The cheerleaders sipped their melon coolers and snubbed me.

I didn't care. I was with Jake, and they weren't. Jealous wannabes.

The bonfire burned down to hot embers, and everybody caravanned over to Dell's house. Jake and I were up front, the leaders.

Jake parked in front of a house. No lights were on. The neighbors' houses on either side were dark, too. Dell was right behind us and pulled his car into the driveway. He sprinted up to the house and turned on some lights, and then he signaled for Jake to help him with the trunk-load of beer. They hefted a case of Bud Light out of the trunk. I grabbed two six-packs of melon coolers, one in each hand, and followed them down a flagstone path to the backyard.

They put the case down next to the back steps, and Dell lit a joint. The marijuana smell was strong and unfamiliar. I'd never seen a joint up close. Dell took a long pull and then offered it to Jake.

Jake shook his head and grabbed a beer from the case. "No thanks, bro."

Dell gulped the smoke down into his lungs and closed his eyes. Then he opened them, holding the orange-tipped joint out to me, his eyebrows raised.

"No, thanks," I said.

Dell exhaled long and low.

"Really good shit. You guys are missin' out," Dell said, shaking his head with disapproval. He opened the back door to the house with his key and flicked on the overhead lights. Jake and I followed him into the kitchen.

Dell's house was similar to mine—older construction, beamed ceilings, wainscoting, and dark, wide-plank wood floors, with an almost identical layout.

We walked down the long hallway from the kitchen to the den. More kids were flooding in through the front door. Someone in the living room put on a Led Zeppelin CD, ultra loud.

"Won't Dell's parents get mad if they find out?" I asked Jake. "Mine would kill me."

"Mine too," Jake grinned. "Not Dell's. His father won't even notice we've been here when they get back. His stepmom won't either. They know how to 'partay' themselves, if you know what I mean."

I shook my head. I really didn't.

"Well, like the first time Dell ever smoked a joint? He stole it from his *dad's* stash. Like that. He and his dad share a joint once in a while and shoot the shit."

"Oh," I said. "Wow." Unimaginable. "Where's his mother?"

I glanced around the den. Unlike my own place-for-everything-and-everything-in-its-place house, Dell's was messy and funky. A dusty, odd clutter of tchotchkes and Asian, African, and old hippie artifacts scattered in a mishmash arrangement decorated their built-in bookshelves.

"Dell's parents got divorced when he was seven. I think his mother lives on the West Coast somewhere. San Francisco maybe? Dell doesn't hear from her much. She married some rich dude a while back. His dad is cool, though," Jake said. "Way cool. Dell gets along good with him. He never gets in Dell's face about anything, even homework and bad grades."

"Isn't it sort of hard on the team, Dell doing drugs and all?"

"Not drugs. Dell only smokes pot, and he stays away from it during the week and before games. He's cool; he's my best friend. He wouldn't let me down." Jake sounded edgy, kind of defensive.

"Right," I agreed. Maybe Dell was as good a friend to Jake as Mel was to me; best friends can sometimes look the other way, so I let it go. Still, to me, pot counted as a drug.

Dell entered the den and walked over to stand next to us. "Dude, I got some of the girls making nachos in the kitchen. They'll be ready soon."

Dell and Jake clinked their beer bottles together and grinned.

The cheerleader girls bounce-stepped in, all busty and blond, their ponytails bobbing high on their heads like golden fountains.

A tall, lanky cheerleader in a red hoodie and dark skinny jeans wrapped her arms around Jake from behind. He turned, laughed, and gave her ponytail a quick tug. She shrieked, and then let him go. Jake drank from his beer while keeping his big-eyed smile on her over the top of the bottle. He took the beer away from his mouth and whispered something in her ear. The girl hooted and shoved his chest with the flat of her hand.

My heartbeat quickened. Was Jake flirting with her? Was he? She glossed over me with spiteful eyes and walked out of the den.

Jake saw me watching her. "Hey, come on, don't get all freaked. The cheerleaders are OK. Once they know you, they'll be cool."

Dell smiled. "Even if they're not, I, for one, am very pleased to make your acquaintance, Ms. Kara." He nodded his head in the direction of the lanky girl and poked Jake in the ribs. "Same ol', same ol'. Cherry Creek High can get sadly boring by senior year. New blood is all good."

"You got that right, bro." Jake smiled and tucked his hand under my chin. "OK, beautiful? Ignore 'em. That's an order."

I focused on his fantastic face and smiled back. "OK. I will."

More kids piled into the den, crowding in until it overflowed. The hallway was full too. I began to worry about the noise, the neighbors, and someone calling the cops. My worst fear was getting caught and my parents finding out. Definitely the end of Jake and me. I stole a nervous glance at my watch.

"Hey, you OK? Want me to take you home?" Jake asked.

"I'm sorry, it's kind of late. Would you mind?"

"No prob." Jake put his arm around me and punched Dell's shoulder.

"Dude, we're outta here."

"You're gonna miss some excellent nachos."

"Kara's parents aren't as cool as yours. We gotta fly."

Dell laughed. "Nobody's parents are as cool as mine."

They high-fived each other, and Dell wandered off toward the kitchen and his nachos. Jake and I made our way through the packed-full house and out into the night.

Sitting in Jake's car, I thought about Dell and felt kind of sad for him. Maybe my parents were too strict, but at least they cared about what I did and where I was.

On the way home, Jake cranked up Bob Marley and began to sing along with the CD, really soft. I smiled to myself. Not only was Jake sensitive and cool, he was mature. Like, he was able to read my mind about being out too late, and he never made me feel embarrassed about it either.

Jake pulled into the alley behind my house and parked the car. My house was dark. I wanted Jake to kiss me, but he slid right out his door and walked around the car to open mine.

Opened my door. A gentleman, too. How could my father not like that?

Jake put his hand out to me and pulled me out of the front seat. We held hands and walked to the edge of my driveway.

"Did you have fun, Ms. Kara?"

"Yes, it was great!" I whispered, sure my father could hear me across the lawn and through several walls.

"There's an away game next weekend, so I won't be around. Do you think you can make it out for a party a week from Saturday? A mondo house in Cherry Creek Village. It's gonna be awesome for sure."

"Yeah, I think so. Sounds good."

"All right. We'll coordinate and figure out your escape plan later."

"Night." Jake leaned down and kissed my cheek. He fixed a smile on me and back-stepped toward his car.

After he drove away I raced across the backyard, climbed up the lattice, over the roof, through the window, and into my room.

Everything was just the way I'd left it. The fake-pillow me was still tucked into my bed, "asleep."

"Yes," I whispered. Home-free.

Every girl in Denver would kill to go out with Jake Dodson. But he'd picked me. He wanted me. There was no way my parents were going to blow this for me.

No possible way.

Welcome to My Pitiful World

My head still full of the bonfire, Dell's party, and Jake, I climbed the steps of the bus and smiled at Iris.

"My, Kara, you look extra pretty today," Iris said.

Iris had been driving the Saint U's bus since I was in seventh grade. She knew each one of us by name. I grinned. I felt pretty too.

Mel flagged me down from her seat near the back. The bus jerked forward and continued to cruise down Logan Avenue. Steadying myself on the seat backs, I made my way along the rubber-treaded aisle and plopped down next to Mel. Her geometry book was open on her lap.

"Quiz today. I hate this shit. Tell me, what new meaning is the isosceles triangle going to bring to my life?"

"None?"

"Exactimundo. So, I've decided. I'm having a sleepover for my birthday next weekend."

"Which night?"

"Friday. Oh, right. Are you going out with Jake again?"

"No, they have an away game next weekend. But we're going out the week after, on Saturday. One of his friends is throwing a mondo party in Cherry Creek Village."

"Whoa, Cherry Creek Village. Cool and *rich* friends. Impressive." But Mel's so-readable face said "Ugh."

I'd kind of ditched Mel these last few weeks. Jake was all I could think about, talk about, and dream about. Mel and I never mentioned what had happened to our friendship since Jake. The whole situation kind of hung out between us like a bad smell.

"You act like you hate him, Mel."

Mel's dark, unplucked eyebrows lifted. She never wore makeup, only clear lip gloss.

"I don't hate him," Mel quipped. "I just think he's kind of an arrogant asshole, OK?"

We laughed, sort of, and I let it slide. Mel was jealous because I'd escaped Saint Ursula's hellhole of social retardation, and she hadn't. Maybe she never would.

I left Mel to her geometry cram and thought about Jake's incredible eyes all the way to school.

The bus stopped and we got off, another boring and repressive day ahead of us. Saint Ursula's Academy for Girls was ninety-five years old. They hadn't bought new desks in the last fifty years, possibly more.

There was this myth about Saint Ursula and the eleven thousand virgins—that they were all martyred because they wouldn't deny their faith in Jesus. Actually, if it was true at all, it was probably only eleven. In religion class, we learned the Biblical historians' hypothesis that a copyist mistakenly interpreted the M in "11 M" from the ancient text as the Roman numeral for a thousand, when it really stood for "martyrs." With mistakes like that, how could you know what to believe? In my opinion, studying the history of the saints was a bore and who really cared.

The Ursuline order of nuns was founded for the education of young women. They had about a zillion girls schools all over the world. Lucky me, living near one of them.

At Saint Ursula's, we still had to wear the same exact uniforms they'd had when my mother went to Saint U's, forever ago. Ugly, blue plaid, pleated skirts; white polyester blouses; and blue blazers with the blue and gold Saint Ursula's emblem on the pocket. Ugh. Our spring uniforms were pathetic, too. Pastel blue or white blouses with blah beige below-the-knee skirts.

The only good news was that there were no boys around to see us in our hideous polyester attire. Mel said uniforms were a metaphor for what the school wanted us to be ... the same. Xerox copies of virtuous girls prepared by Saint U's to file out into the world, tamed and obedient.

Mel and I scuffed our feet along the blue and green linoleum-tiled floor, passing two pictures of the Sacred Heart, a huge statue of the Blessed Mother, and another of Saint Ursula in the puke-green cinder-block hallway on our way to homeroom. A multitude of saints watched over us at Saint Ursula's. In every room and hallway, their suffering, porcelain faces stared us down. Even the bathrooms had crucifixes.

Sister Elaine, our homeroom and global studies teacher, was the meanest nun in the whole school. Mel called her Evil Elaine because her face was constantly set in a creepy grimace, and her eyes flitted around the room like a crazy person's while she taught.

Evil was even more in fret mode than usual when we got to homeroom. Teary-eyed, Sister was waiting for everyone to "settle down" as she called it. Mel and I took our seats.

"Girls, when we say our morning prayer, I want you to remember all the little babies that were buried yesterday. All those innocent little beings who were put to rest."

Mel's hand shot up. "Babies? What babies?"

Sister Elaine's face turned scarlet. Big blue veins popped out on her neck.

"Don't you read the newspaper, Melanie? Aren't you keeping up with your current events?" Spit sprayed out of her mouth, hitting the tops of Jenna's and Dakota's heads. Poor unfortunates. They were alphabetically challenged with *A* through *D* names, so their desks were in the front row. Mel and I were lucky middle-row sitters.

Mel lifted her shoulders in silence, but it seemed to me like she wanted to scream.

Samantha raised her hand—she always did. You could tell time by the way she sucked up. She was a loser and a half. Nobody liked her.

"Sister is referring to the burial of the fetal ashes from the abortion clinics at a church north of here called ...," Samantha stalled and flushed. She'd forgotten the name.

"Saint Jude's," Sister Elaine prodded.

"Oh, right. They buried the remains from some miscarriages too. There was an article about it in the *Post* on Saturday."

Sister Elaine's eyes shone, the kind of shine psychopath's eyes have in horror movies. Samantha received a gargantuan smile from Sister, displaying her mouthful of yellowed teeth to the class. Samantha would get an A in global studies for the semester, no doubt.

"Yes, Samantha, that's correct. All those tiny lost souls. As Catholics, girls, we know that, not only is abortion a sin, it is also murder. The Church does not condone this taking of innocent lives and never will."

Mel's hand flew up again. Sister wouldn't call on her, so Mel just shouted out her question. "What about Catholics for Choice?"

Sister Elaine registered shock, as if she'd been slapped. "They are severely misguided. According to papal law, they should be excommunicated."

Sister Elaine bowed her head and circled a pointed finger in the air for us to do the same.

"Let us pray. Dearest Lord, we ask you to oversee all our endeavors this day. We ask that you keep us in your Sacred Heart and hold us in your Divine Light. Please bless all the small souls done away with through such selfish ignorance. Help people everywhere to be mindful of how precious the gift of life truly is. Help them to realize that all children belong to God. Amen."

The "Amens" of the class were not whole-hearted enough for Sister Elaine. Her dark eyes scanned the classroom, sharp as splintered glass.

The "Amens" came again, louder. But Mel said nothing; she remained defiantly silent.

The bell rang, and we all grabbed our books and headed for our first classes.

"She is so full of it," Mel growled, rushing past the life-sized portrait of Saint Ursula outside our homeroom.

"You mean that prayer?"

"All of it. I knew about the buried fetuses. Mom and I read that article and talked about how lame it was. We should probably be excommunicated."

"Your mother is pro-choice? Really? I didn't know."

"Yeah, she doesn't talk about it much. Maybe she's afraid I'll be expelled."

We shared a smirk.

"That could be a good thing. Take me with you!" I said.

The bell signaling the start of classes rang.

"Definitely. See you at lunch."

Mel ducked into geometry, and I headed to my history class across the hall.

I loved the way Mel spoke her mind about things. I admired her for it. She wasn't afraid; sometimes I wished I had her nerve.

Hamburger day.

The food at Saint Ursula's was a lot better than the social opportunities. No doubt.

The cafeteria line was already a mile long when I got there. Mel and Dakota were up near the front. They waved me over and let me cut. Jenna and Maura were there, too. Maura moved to Denver from Santa Monica last year. She edged Samantha out as the super-brain of our class, putting me in the number three slot.

We loaded our trays and asked for extra cheese and green chile on our burgers. Mel got a scoop of the fiery hot stuff on top of her fries too. We stopped at the condiment table for relish, onions, the works.

The five of us made our way to our usual spot in the corner by the windows. The sun always beat down on our table before lunch period, so it was nice and warm by the time we got there. My last class before lunch was on the north side of the building, a veritable deep freeze. I set my tray down and laid my hands flat on the toasty Formica for a quick thaw.

Middle school kids ate at a different time than the upper school. Thank God. It was bad enough that we had to share the building with them, but nobody wanted to hear their giggles and squeals while eating and trying to have an intelligent conversation.

Mel put her tray down next to mine in mid-discussion with Dakota, still all revved up about Evil Elaine's morning drama.

"All that shit about the 'little lost souls.' What an extremist, a frigging nut case."

Dakota gave Mel a nod. "Right. A woman's body, a woman's choice." Dakota wasn't afraid to call herself a feminist even though it was not exactly cool or something that most St. U's girls knew or cared much about. Tall with wavy auburn hair and hazel eyes, Dakota turned heads without even trying, but never paid much attention to what boys liked or didn't like. She always talked about being an individual, and being true to herself. She couldn't have cared less what guys thought—about her, or anything.

Mel was really into feminism too. She and Dakota were totally on the same page there. They had both read *The Da Vinci Code* about a million times—another book that was forbidden at Saint U's, like *Gossip Girls* and the *Twilight* series. Mel and Dakota fantasized about the Church rediscovering the Divine Feminine and about a woman being pope someday. In my opinion, when Hell froze over the pope would still be an old, white male and the Divine Feminine still unrecognized.

"The parental consent law in Colorado is totally bogus," Maura, the perpetual California snob, gloated. "They don't have that in California." Maura stuffed some fries into her mouth, accidentally leaving a smear of ketchup on her chin. I didn't tell her to wipe it off.

"Yeah, like, at sixteen? You can get a license to drive here. My mom always says, 'Why is a girl allowed to drive but can't get birth control if she needs it?' That's so harsh," Dakota added.

Dakota's mother had offered condoms to any kids who needed them in the eighth grade sex ed class she taught at the middle school. She almost got fired for it.

Mel's head bounced up and down like a bobblehead doll. "Sure, a girl is old enough to run someone over, to kill or permanently maim them with a two-ton vehicle, but she can't get the pill without her parents' permission!" Mel was outraged, over the top.

No way my father would let me drive when I turned sixteen. I could drive when I was eighteen, at the earliest—another one of his ridiculous rules. If he ever found out about Jake and me, it might turn into age twenty-one. Or never.

"What if it *is* murder, though, like Sister Elaine says?" Jenna asked, her light blue eyes all watery and wide. Jenna was the pretty featherhead, she fit right into all the stereotypical notions suggested by the term "dumb blonde." The naïve one, Jenna was ready to believe anyone about anything, anytime.

"Jeez. No. It's not murder." Mel slapped her hand on the table so hard that some of our plastic lunch plates shook. She and Dakota exchanged glances and rolled their eyes.

"Oh! What if they all went to limbo?" Jenna seemed genuinely sad at the thought.

"Limbo?" Mel and Dakota shared a laugh.

"Jenna," Mel groaned, "Limbo is so second grade. Come *on*."

"Didn't the pope do away with that whole concept?" Maura chimed in, her mouth half-full.

Of course there was no response. Our table couldn't have cared less about limbo or entering into a discussion about the current changes in Church dogma.

"Now there's Plan B, and RU-486 is legal in all fifty states." Dakota ticked these reproductive rights victories off on two fingers and gobbled a French fry.

"About freaking time." Mel and Dakota high-fived their agreement.

Mel fast-forwarded right into the Catholics for Choice thing. Mel didn't mention her mother's being a member, but she and Dakota really dug into the topic. Maura and Jenna added their pro and con thoughts between bites.

I munched my burger and cheese fries and had no opinions to share about choice, buried fetuses, any of it.

My head was full of Jake.

Good Catholics/Bad Catholics?

Nothing made me want to sleep in on Sundays more than the thought of going to Mass. What a total waste of a day off, a boring, time-consuming drone.

Riding in the back seat of my father's car, I imagined Jake sprawled out across his bed, his feet hanging off one end, with a tangle of sheets covering his long, incredible body. I smiled to myself. Thank God my parents couldn't read my mind. They had no clue I'd snuck out with him or that we already had plans for the next time.

My father pulled into the congested church parking lot. Mel and her brother were halfway up the church steps, walking next to their mother, Sherry. I wondered if Mom knew that Sherry belonged to the Catholics for Choice thing. I'd never tell.

We took aisle seats in a pew toward the middle of the church. I went in last so I could lean against the armrest at the end. Mel's family was sitting two rows ahead of us.

The worst part about Mass was the sermon. Our pastor, Father Miller, was long-winded to an extreme. Determined to make sure everyone would get the various points he wanted to make, he found twenty or thirty different ways to hammer each one of them in.

When he began his boring blah-blahs, I began my mental retreat. Putting my thumb under my chin for balance, I let the flat of my open palm rest against my cheek to shield my face from my parents' view. I supported my right arm with my left hand, and leaned my left elbow on the armrest, then turned my head in the direction of the pulpit, pretending total concentration.

Father Miller was not even an interesting visual. Bald on top with medium-length white fluff on the sides and back of his head, he had ruddy cheeks and thick, square, black-framed glasses that magnified his eyes into a Yoda-like bulge.

Eyes closed, the nasal buzz of the sermon eased into my left ear, swooshed across my brain, and exited my right. In and out, in and out—the rhythm became almost soothing. After a few minutes, my mind was tuned out and my mid-Mass nap had begun.

"So, *how* does this happen, you may ask ..."

The booming upsurge of Father Miller's voice jarred me awake.

"How do we as humans get so *far away* from our conscience, from the basic principles of right and *wrong*?"

Father Miller was using his harsh, guilt-inducing tone.

"So, here we sit, at Sunday Mass, calling ourselves good Catholics. How is it that some of us dare to question our dogma, our faith, the will of the Holy See itself, in this important matter? I do not understand. No, I cannot."

I glanced sideways at my parents. Their eyes were fixated on Father Miller. I sat up straighter, adjusted my skirt, hoping the bulk of the sermon was over.

"How is it that some can justify this holocaust of innocent souls day after day throughout this country?" Father Miller's eyes darted back and forth, thrilling to the sound of his own words.

A man coughed a few pews behind me, the barky sound echoed up into the vastness of the cathedral ceiling. A quiet sigh escaped from my mother. She grasped my father's hand, and he held it across his knee.

With a long sweep of his arm, Father Miller cut through the space in front of him, his vestments flapping in the rush of air. His bony finger pointed down the center aisle and then swung left and right, skewering each person who sat before him.

"I tell you this: The only way to determine where you stand in your humanity and in your Catholicism during these dark, dark times is to ask yourself whether or not you are at war. A war that is right here under our noses every day—the war against abortion on demand."

Father let his words sink into the congregation for a long beat and then adjusted his microphone and leaned into it.

"Even though you may attend Mass and receive the sacraments regularly, if you are not opposing the proliferation of abortion in some way, some meaningful way, no matter how small, you are doing a disservice to yourself and to Catholics everywhere. You are, by your silence, in a very significant way, an accomplice ... to murder."

I glanced over at Mel. Her eyes were crossed, she was pinching her nose and smirking for my benefit. The fearless rebel. Only I saw her. The rest of the congregation was riveted to Father Miller; all ears tuned to the rising fervor of his words.

Father stood for a long moment, his huge, distorted eyes scrutinizing everyone in the church through his thick glasses, silently broadcasting his stern message—don't dare disagree with me, or you are not a good Catholic!

People were nodding and crossing themselves. My mother did, too.

"God wants us all to defend and preserve His most precious gift, the gift of life. One of the best ways we can help, can protect His precious gift, is at the ballot box, through our votes. This is a powerful tool, and we, as good Catholics, need to exercise it well, to make sure our voices are heard. We must continue to be soldiers of our Lord. Now, and always."

Father's crimson and gold vestments flowed regally behind him as he climbed down from the pulpit and strode back to the altar to finish saying the Mass.

Mel was ready to blow. She was nudging her mother, but getting zero reaction. Her mother shook her head, keeping her face forward and her back straight. Mel's little brother yawned and stretched, oblivious.

Mass finally ended. The congregation exploded from the church like a jostling herd of cattle eager to escape a crowded pen. Brushing against one another and nodding acknowledgments, the glut of Catholics moved toward a single goal—the parking lot.

Tons of girls from Saint U's were there. All of them trained to be good girls, good Catholics, every one of them probably as bored as I was.

Mel sidled up next to me. "God, let me out of here. Talk about the dark times, he's making them pitch black!"

Sherry touched Mel's arm, her eyes gently cautious. Mel went quiet. Sherry smiled at me.

"Hey, Kara, how's school going this year?"

"Fine, fine. Status quo, I guess." As mothers go, Sherry was definitely on the cool side of things.

My mother waved to Sherry and motioned for me to catch up to them.

Mel poked my arm. "What about the global studies project?"

"Haven't started it. Call me later."

We said good-bye, navigating our separate ways through the teeming parking lot.

"Maybe I should get involved with DLA again…what do you think?" my mother was asking my father as I reached the car. "At least I could make some phone calls or help with fundraising for that pro-life candidate. Oh, I can't believe I'm forgetting his name … "

"Bruce Statler," my father said, unlocking the doors with a beep from the remote. Mom held the front seat up, and I climbed in back.

They were talking about the Defense of Life Association—DLA for short. Because my mother didn't have a paying job, she volunteered. She had helped out at the DLA a few years ago. My mother left her job as an interior designer for her pathetic stay-at-home-mom existence when I was born. I wished she would work, at least part time; I envied all my friends their latchkey freedom.

"It's up to you." Dad got into the car and put his key into the ignition. "But I thought you'd become disenchanted with them. You said they were too virulent and aggressive, that you didn't want to get involved with their picketing of women's clinics and the like."

"Some of their ways made me uncomfortable, yes, but I believe they've stopped all that now."

I flashed on my eight-year-old self sitting next to my mother in a brightly lit office downtown, stuffing envelopes with pro-life mailers—"Choose Life, Choose Life."

"I realize that," my father said as he backed slowly out of the parking space, "but, come on, Maggie, do we have to jump at every word Father Miller utters? We're doing just fine. Kara's at Saint Ursula's. We go to Mass, communion, all the church fund-raisers ..." His tone was sour. Dad tapped his thumb against his black leather-sleeved steering wheel.

Mom saw our neighbor Mrs. Moriarity walking by and waved to her.

"Can we get Krispy Kreme on the way home?" I asked. I needed a sugar fix for my PMS—Post-Mass Syndrome.

"I think that can definitely be arranged," Dad said, waiting his turn to get through the tangle of cars. He put his hand on Mom's shoulder and massaged it.

Mom turned to him and put her hand over his. "You're right, I probably don't need to start all that up again. It really was a huge commitment."

Relief. I'd already planned to plead homework overload if Mom wanted me to go downtown and stuff envelopes again. The women there were all right; some of them were from our parish and some were from other churches. They gave me fresh-baked chocolate chip muffins and Coke. I liked them OK, but sometimes I felt weird, like they wanted me to be just like them and think just like them.

A calm silence filled the Mercedes as we cruised toward our Krispy Kreme destination.

Jake was lucky. He wasn't Catholic, and his parents weren't even very religious. Jake was free to do whatever he pleased without sin, damnation, or guilt to get in his way.

Slumbering Innocents

For her birthday, I bought Mel a book called *The Expected One*. I heard the author interviewed on NPR, and it sounded kind of like the *Da Vinci Code* but even more controversial. Secret scrolls, Mary Magdalene's relationship with Jesus ... it was sure to be banned by the Church and at school, too. Mel would love it.

Mel was a total activist, always talking up social and political issues and trying to make people conscious and aware and all that. She was dead sure of her beliefs, but her activism didn't exactly make her a male magnet, in my opinion.

Mel had always been a little on the chunky side, and she never bothered much about her looks. A little blush and mascara would've helped, but Mel couldn't have cared less. She had more important things on her mind than makeup, and more than her share of spunk and spirit. In my view, if Mel cut down on pizza and chile-cheese fries and toned down the feminist-activist thing, maybe she could meet a guy, too.

Jake didn't like feminists and said they all hated men. I knew he wouldn't like Mel even if he got to know her.

Mel and I had been best friends since forever. We had made our First Communion together in the second grade, and our Confirmation in fifth. We'd both gotten our periods the same week during the sixth grade and began our hideous time at Saint Ursula's Academy, side by side, in middle school.

Mel's father was killed in a car accident when we were in the seventh grade, hit by a drunk driver. Mel had been really close to her dad, and she changed after that. She'd always been tough, but her father's death made Mel even more rebellious and outspoken. It was like she had nothing to lose. At her dad's memorial, Mel and I made a vow: We swore to each other that we would never drink alcohol and sealed it with a pinky promise.

When I needed to unload about the super-strict aspects of my home life, I could trust Mel. She knew how to listen and how to keep quiet about things, too. She knew how I felt about my father, how I couldn't even breathe around him anymore without getting into trouble or being grounded, and that being at home felt like jail. Mel was the only one of my friends who really understood.

On this birthday, Mel was going to be "sweet sixteen," and she had never been kissed. After years of being cloistered at Saint U's, I'd be the same when I hit sixteen—unless Jake kissed me.

But I knew he would. There was plenty of time—my birthday was three long months away.

Jake. Everything about him was awesome. I loved to watch him play basketball, to watch him drive, and to see him standing under the street light in the alley behind my house.

When we were younger, Mel and I used to wonder how girls got boy-crazy, how they could waste so much time and energy obsessing about guys. Now, I knew. I'd never had such intense feelings. Ever. I wanted to know everything about Jake. To read him like a favorite book, the kind that was so good you never wanted it to end.

Jake was the only exciting thing in my life. Because of him, I felt interesting and cool.

Mel's favorite pizza was pineapple with bacon and extra cheese. She said pineapple on pizza was an acquired taste. Yeah it was, and Mel was the only one at the party who'd acquired it. Thank God her mother had ordered two other kinds.

One length of the kitchen counter was covered with dairy products. Mel wanted make-your-own milkshakes instead of a cake. Cartons of dark chocolate, dulce de leche, vanilla, and mint chip ice cream sat next to a gallon of milk and plastic bottles of caramel, marshmallow, and chocolate malt syrups. The final touches were lined up near the blender: chocolate sprinkles, nuts, and a can of whipped cream.

Jake and his friends would have a total laugh fest if they saw me making milkshakes at a sleep over like a twelve-year-old.

It was strange. Mel's party was a total do-over of her seventh-grade one, right down to the milkshakes. I enjoyed a good milkshake as much as anyone, but for my sixteenth birthday I wanted to go out to dinner, with Jake, somewhere really sophisticated and romantic. Maybe he would even be allowed to pick me up at my house, at the front door, no sneaking out. The thought made me smile.

No way I'd have a slumber party with a bunch of girls. Since I'd met Jake, Mel and all my Saint U friends seemed immature and childish to me. I was outgrowing them and didn't like feeling that way. But when I thought about Jake and about being with him at the party next weekend, I felt all happy.

After committing total gluttony in the kitchen, we all settled down in Mel's den to watch movies and fully absorb our carbs. Mel pulled a bunch of DVDs from the shelf below the big-screen TV and spread them out on the rug. "Choose," she said. The rest of the girls descended on the pile of DVDs like a pack of starving wolves on a downed deer. Their voices ran together in a shrill explosion of words.

"What about *Grease*? John Travolta has the best buns in that one."

"No. *Devil's Advocate*! I love Keanu. He's so hot."

"He's gay ... isn't he?"

"I don't know. Does that mean he's *not* hot? Jeez."

"Oooh, *Great Expectations*! I love Ethan Hawke. Can you believe he dumped Uma Thurman?"

"I thought she dumped him."

"No way."

"Way. He's a scammer."

"Most men are."

"Oh yeah they are."

Ugh. Their inane blabber was so middle school. I was bored and couldn't have cared less what movie they picked, whose buns were cutest. All I wanted was for next Saturday night to be here, ASAP.

"What do any of you know about public school girls?" I asked.

"Oooh, I forgot. Kara's too good for this female-only soiree. She's going out with Mr. Cherry Creek," Maura teased.

Her precious GPA and getting into an Ivy mattered much more to her than guys, pimples, or carb counting for that matter. Her use of words like "soiree" made me want to puke.

"Still a virgin, Kara?" Maura pressed.

What a snot! I blushed. "Shut up."

"Uh-oh, better get your tiny heinie to confession."

"At least mine's tiny," I snapped.

That shut Maura's big mouth. At least for the moment.

"Jake's a hottie, definitely awesome and all, but like, hasn't he had, like, a zillion girlfriends?" Jenna asked Dakota, like I wasn't sitting right there. Dakota shrugged her reply, too busy searching through the DVDs to answer.

Just imagining Jake with another girl made me prickly.

Mel stood up and imitated Sister Elaine's rigid posture and stern facial expression to perfection. "Remember girls, the only method that really works is … abstinence!"

Like Evil Elaine would ever talk to us about sex or birth control. As if. Still, everyone cracked up, minus me.

"Pathetic losers," I mumbled. They were jealous of me, all of them.

"Whoa. Aren't we harsh?" Maura batted her stubby, caked with blue mascara eyelashes at me. I enjoyed a brief fantasy of strangling her, cramming her fat, pimply self into a box, and FedExing it back to smoggy California. A mortal sin? Yeah. A black mark on my soul? Sure. But wouldn't it be a kind of humanitarian act, too— wouldn't it make the world a better place?

My world at least.

"Hey, chill, will you? I'm celebrating a birthday here," Mel said and slipped *Great Expectations* into the DVD player. She leaned back against the sofa, taking charge of the group with the remote.

"Oh God, like, speaking of virgins? There was this club at the middle school where my mother works? Like, you had to have sex with a high school boy to get in. A bunch of girls got expelled, and one of them even got pregnant!" Dakota squealed, all excited.

"No way! Saint U's middle school?" Jenna asked, slack jawed.

"No, dummy, public. Where my *mom* works. I heard her talking about it with one of the other counselors on the phone."

A chorus of dissing voices grew.

"Must be hideous for your mom working there."

"Double bad!"

"Public school girls are so slutty."

"They can't say no."

"They're losers. Used by boys and don't even know it."

Unable to handle another second of their infantile, ignorant, depressing chatter, I grabbed my purse and stood up.

"Happy birthday, Mel. See you on Monday."

Mel was stunned. Maura swiped the remote from her and turned up the volume. Everyone was zonked out from carb overload and engrossed in *Great Expectations* as I walked out.

Mel trailed after me.

"Kara, come on, don't go. Please? You're my best friend. It won't be the same if you leave."

"Why do they always have to dis everything and everyone?"

"They're jealous, that's all. Envy is only a venial sin." Mel poked my arm and winked. She can usually make me smile with her Catholic jokes.

"Come on, don't take it personally. Jenna was telling Maura what a hottie she thinks Jake is right before you got here."

I softened. "Well. At least she has taste."

"Stay, OK? There's a hot sex scene coming up, absolutely torrid, where Gwyneth takes all her clothes off." Mel had her arm around my shoulder, guiding me back toward the den.

"What about Ethan?"

"Him, too. Cute enough buns, but in my view, Travolta's are superior."

"But not naked."

"Oh well, what do you expect? *Grease* takes place in the fifties!"

Mel and I walked back into the den and settled down with the others. Ethan was about to kiss Gwyneth.

I guess he was kind of hot.

Pro and Con Rhythms

"Thanks, hon. Once you get a rhythm going, you'll whip through these flyers in no time," Mom said. She dialed the first number from her list and headed into the kitchen.

"Regina? … Hi. Maggie MacNeill. … Fine, fine. Everything's great, and you? … Good, glad to hear it. The reason I'm calling is that I've gotten involved with the DLA again, and we're doing our best to get Bruce Statler elected."

Because it was a Saturday afternoon, my mother didn't buy the I-have-too-much-homework line. She said I had to help do the mailing while she did the phone calling. Jean Moriarity had given her a list of fifty-plus people to call.

I set down my snack, Coke, nacho-style Doritos, and sour cream dip on a place mat by the pile of flyers on our dining room table. A stack of empty envelopes, a dampened sponge in a saucer, and sheets of address labels were set in a line next to the flyers.

"Statler's pro-life, and he has a fabulous track record," Mom chirped. "I just know you'll be impressed. He'll be speaking and then doing a Q-and-A at a DLA gathering at Jean Moriarity's on the twenty-eighth. Father Miller will be there, too. I'm hoping you and Paul will be able to make it. You can? Great, I'll put you down! Thanks. See you soon."

I picked up one of the Statler flyers. Bruce Statler had brown hair and eyes and thin lips. His tie was too tightly knotted. His perfectly straight teeth were set in a fake smile.

Underneath his photo, there was a brief bio about him and the highlights of his past political achievements. Underneath that, in big red letters, it read:

PLANNED PARENTHOOD = FETAL DEATH CAMPS
STOP THE ABORTION HOLOCAUST!
VOTE BRUCE STATLER

At the bottom of the flyer was a small, extremely magnified picture of a thumb-sucking fetus and next to it, four words: "I have rights too!"

Harsh. Much harsher than the ones I remembered the DLA sending out when I was eight. Those were all text and no graphics. I folded the flyer in three and shoved it into an envelope.

Our phone rang, and Mom picked up. "Hello? … Oh, hi, honey. How's it going?"

My father was calling from his office. He often worked on weekends, too. He was a workaholic, but at least his many hours at the job gave me breathing room at home.

"Oh, not much. Kara has homework to do, and I was just reading. What time do you think you'll be home? Yes, all right. Good. See you then. Bye."

Mom had lied about what we were doing. An outright lie. And right in front of me, too. Did she think I couldn't hear her from fifteen feet away? Maybe she was afraid my father would be jealous because so much of her time and energy was going to Statler? Weird, no doubt, but no way I was going to ask Mom about it.

I heard her hang up and dial the next number on her list.

"Jane? ... Hi, it's Maggie MacNeill. How are you doing? ... Good, good. We're all fine, yes. Couldn't be better ... "

Mel hated Statler. No way I'd tell her that I'd helped with my mother's mailers. If she found out, our friendship would end in a heartbeat. She'd pass me in the hallways at school without so much as a nod. That's how much Mel hated Statler.

But from my mother's point of view, we were just being good Catholics.

"No, Kara's a sophomore this year. Hard to believe, isn't it?" My mother sounded happy, the way she always did when she felt she was being "productive."

I set my iPod on shuffle, took a sip of Coke, downed a few chips with sour cream, and started in on the pile in front of me.

I didn't care much about Bruce Statler or his campaign goals. But stuffing envelopes would help the time pass faster, and that was my goal. In only seven hours, Jake would be in the alley, waiting to pick me up for the party.

As my mother had predicted, I got into a rhythm. Fold into thirds, stuff in the envelope, rub the flap across the damp sponge, seal, and put in the pile beside me.

It was going fast; I had more than twenty already on the finished pile. I decided it would be easiest to put the address labels on at the end.

I turned up the volume on my iPod and set my pace to Bob Marley. As I folded and stuffed, my mind reeled through a fantasy preview of the Cherry Creek party, how awesome it would be, and all the cool kids who'd be there. Anyone who was anyone would be there.

And so would I.

I could hardly wait for the most fun night of my monotonous flat line of a life to begin.

All Partied Out

Jake's friend Rob had the party. He'd been captain of Cherry Creek's team last year when Jake was a junior. Even though his grades were pitiful, Rob had gotten a full basketball scholarship to the University of Denver.

"Buffalo Soldier" was blasting when Jake and I walked in. That made me grin, like they were playing it especially for us. Because of Jake, I listened to Bob Marley all the time.

Rob's family lived in Cherry Creek Village in a six-bedroom house with a triple garage. It was wall-to-wall kids that night. Rob's parents were away on a two-week cruise in the Caribbean, and his younger sister was staying with their grandparents.

No way could I imagine my father and mother taking off on a Caribbean vacation or leaving me with the house to myself.

All the guys from the basketball team, a ton of seniors from Cherry Creek, and lots of Rob's college friends from DU were there. It was definitely an older crowd. I was probably the only high school sophomore.

The same girls who had dissed me at the bonfire dissed me again.

They were pathetic. I didn't care; Jake was holding my hand, navigating me through the crowded living room.

A few couples were wrapped around one another, python-like, on the sofa. Kids talking, smoking, and drinking overflowed into the entryway from the candlelit living room. Halfway through the dining room, I almost tripped over a tangle of legs. The top half of the couple was hidden beneath the dining room table, a long, damask tablecloth providing them with a curtain of privacy. I was staring at their shoeless, in-motion legs that sprawled out onto the Persian rug.

Jake grinned and pulled me around them, through the swinging door, and into the kitchen.

An iced keg of beer sat in the corner with an aluminum tub underneath the spigot to catch drips. Half-empty wine and tequila bottles, wedges of lime, and a salt shaker were strewn along the forest green granite countertop.

A pyramid of small plastic containers full of red and green Jell-O had been erected next to the refrigerator. Jell-O shots. They had vodka in them, or was it gin? A big, blue bottle behind the pyramid said "SKYY," with the word "orange" in script underneath. Vodka, right.

I'd learned a few things about partying since Jake. Real partying, not the make-your-own-milkshake kind.

Jake moved in a different world from mine—the coolest of the cool world. He knew everyone and was invited everywhere.

Four guys were sharing a joint in the corner. Jake called them stoners. One of them was Dell. I held my breath when we passed them.

Jake grabbed a plastic cup from a stack by the keg and poured a beer, tilting the cup and moving the keg handle just so. He had it down to a science. Jake was an expert at getting the most beer into his cup with the least foam. The foam was really called a head. Jake laughed when I'd called it foam at the first party we'd gone to. He thought I was just being cute, and I let him think that. No way would I let on how super sheltered I was.

Jake held the frothy beer out to me.

"No thanks."

He frowned, took a long sip, and wiped a trace of foam from his upper lip. "Your problem is you're wound too tight. There's nothing wrong with having a brew once in a while. Jeez."

"I just don't like beer, that's all."

"You don't like wine either, or Jell-O shots. No beer in them."

Jake took another swallow from his red Solo cup.

I shrugged and looked away, thinking about Mel, her father, and our vow.

"Or weed, how about that? Everybody needs to chill sometimes, Kara."

Jake moved across the kitchen to talk with one of his friends and left me standing alone by the keg. I felt so out of it. I didn't really know anyone at the party besides Jake and Dell.

What if I was wound too tight, like some overprotected baby who needed to grow up? What if Jake stopped liking me and asking me out? What if the only time I ever saw him again was on the sports page of the *Denver Post*?

Jake leaned against the counter and laughed hard, his thick hair falling over one eye. He pushed it back with his hand and then slapped his friend five. More laughs. They toasted with their plastic cups.

Jake. Gorgeous, cool, popular, and totally amazing Jake. I wanted to be his girlfriend more than anything. Anything. I grabbed a Jell-O shot from the pile.

Jake saw me. He turned and smiled. I took the top off and popped the smooth, green shape into my mouth. The vodka tasted sharp, but the Jell-O slid down my throat. Easy. I took another.

Jake's friends clapped and whistled. "Go, girl. All right!"

Jake walked over and put his arm around me, squeezed my shoulders, and pulled me close. "See? She's cool."

Every face in the kitchen zoomed in on me, piercing me. I went from totally invisible to too visible.

I gobbled the second Jell-O shot.

I'm sorry, Mel. Sorry.

Jake topped off his beer.

Dell passed the joint off to his friends and left the corner. He set the timer on the face of the microwave and nodded at Jake. Three guys from the Cherry Creek team started to count, their eyes on Jake.

"Fifteen, fourteen, thirteen, twelve, eleven, ten, nine, eight, seven, go dude, go, go!! Six, five, four … all right!"

Jake chugged the beer down in a flash, finishing the last of it before they made it past five. I ate two more Jell-O shots. The Jell-O was shiny, bouncy.

Jake winked at me. He took a piece of lime, sprinkled salt in the crook of his hand, poured himself a shot of tequila, and downed it.

I picked up another shot, a red one. The pyramid pile had lost its peak. Was this four or five? I'd lost count and didn't care.

Dell set the timer and nodded at me. "Go Kara, go, go, go!!" The same three guys began to count.

I scooped the Jell-O out and swallowed it before they got to ten. Jake slapped me five and moved over to the keg for more beer.

Jake pulled a shot from the bottom row and the remains of the pyramid pile toppled down onto the counter. He popped the Jell-O out of its tiny tub and bit half off. He put the other half into my mouth, like a priest giving me communion. I could hardly taste the vodka.

We smiled at each other and bowed for the crowd. Jake's teammates went wild, clapping and hooting. I felt accepted, and cool. Jake smiled big and hugged me close. Jake and me, our own little team.

The I'm-so-hot cheerleader girl from Dell's party was leaning against the counter by the kitchen door, watching us. Mocking me with her eyes. Jake took my hand and led me out of the kitchen, past her jealous face. My eyes mocked her right back.

Jake and I cruised through the living room. Couples were hooking up everywhere. Half-empty drink cups and melted-down candles were scattered around the room. Someone put a *Best of the Stones* CD on way loud. "Miss You" was playing when we found a place to sit on an overstuffed sofa.

I tasted beer on Jake's mouth when he pulled me close and kissed me for the first time. I didn't care; I felt so amazing being with Jake at a cool party, my arms wrapped around him, him holding me. Claiming me.

Jake kissed me again. It felt good, really good. I was loose and soft all over. Jake had no clue what a novice I was.

The living room was jam-packed, but I felt like we were alone. Jake and me, in our own little universe.

Jake's eyes seemed even more incredible in the candlelight, luminous and bright. His hair was soft and thick when I touched it. I was glad the coach let him keep it long. I'd never felt this happy before, this alive. Even though we'd only been out a few times, I knew I loved him. I wanted to love him forever.

"Let's go upstairs. Want to?" Jake asked, really gentle and soft, into my ear. My ear was all hot where his lips brushed against it. My hands were on the back of his neck, and I pressed myself against him, really close, and whispered "OK" into his ear. It felt so romantic, like we were in a movie.

"Angie" was playing as we climbed the stairs. Soft pools of light fell from the amber etched-glass sconces onto a runner in the long hallway. The bedroom doors were all shut, and muffled sounds and voices leaked out from behind them.

I heard Jake's crowd cheering someone on, using the timer to clock someone else chugging down a brew.

Jake knocked on a door, and then he opened it.

"Get out!" a guy shouted from the pitch dark room. I heard a girl laugh.

"Sorry, dude." Jake banged the door shut and slipped his arm from my shoulders down across my lower back. He tucked his thumb under the waistband of my jeans and touched my bare skin. I smiled up at him, I liked it. Then I tripped on the edge of the rug and Jake caught me. We laughed. Everything seemed hilarious, soft, and hazy.

A couple walked out of a bedroom at the end of the hall. The guy gave Jake a thumbs-up. The girl walking beside him had her blouse on inside out—frayed seams on the outside, backward buttons, the collar half in and half out. It cracked me up.

"D' you see that, her shirt?" I punched Jake's shoulder. My snorts, bordering on guffaws, echoed off the sage-colored walls.

"Ssshhhh," Jake said. "Cool it, OK? Chill." Grabbing my hand, he led me into the empty bedroom and closed the door.

The narrow shapes of two single beds and a tall dresser were somewhat visible in the blackness. A little nightlight glowed dimly from the corner of the room; yellow, red, and black pieces of cut glass shaped into the form of a tiny lighthouse.

"Look! Isn't that so cute?"

"Come here," Jake said and pulled me down onto one of the beds. The spread felt all lumpy and messed up under my back.

Jake's mouth was on mine, kissing me. I was into it and getting pretty good, too. My head was all fuzzy and warm.

Jake pulled my sweater up and touched my stretch bra. He put his hand underneath and moved it up off my breasts. I couldn't believe I was letting him. His touching me felt good, but I worried about being too flat, that he wouldn't like it.

Jake was kissing me, kissing me. It was tender and easy at first, then harder. One hand was on my breast; his other moved down across my stomach.

I really turn him on, I thought, and felt happy and smooth all over. I ran my hand through his hair and kissed him back.

Pants unsnapped, a zipper unzipped; the sounds seemed far away.

"Oh, you feel so good," Jake gasped in my ear, intense.

"Sympathy for the Devil" drifted up from the living room, a pounding surround sound filling the dark air.

Loud, louder.

Another zipper opening. Mine. My jeans.

Jake was tugging at them, pulling them down over my hips and pushing my shirt up, touching me everywhere.

"So good, yeah," he murmured.

I felt dizzy and hot. I reached down to my thigh, feeling for the top of my jeans, but they were down, all the way down. Jake's thigh was naked under my hand.

The elastic of my underwear stung me as it snapped against my bare skin. Jake shoved my underpants over my knees with his foot, pushing them off onto the floor. I lifted my head. His hand was on my chest close to my throat, heavy, pressing me down.

"Wait, stop." I sounded strange, delicate. A dry whisper of a voice, not my own. But Jake was far away, off in his own head. Somewhere that had nothing to do with me at all.

My eyes opened wide, like rising from a deep, deep dream. Waking up.

Across the room I saw the nightlight. The little lighthouse was all blurry, a jumble of tiny colored lights spinning in circles.

"Oh God, Oh God!" Jake panted, pushing himself into me, into me. Sharp and rough. I clenched my jaw against the pain. My breath came out in jagged bursts. My mouth was open, but empty of words. *Stop-No-Don't* spun silently through my brain.

The music was loud, pounding through my ears.

Floating.

I floated up, up, outside of my body until I was out, swimming through the darkness toward the glow of the cut-glass lighthouse.

Watching Jake heaving his massive body on top of me, into me.

Watching the silent, unmoving me. Underneath.

My sweaty face felt stuck to the leather seat of a car. Engulfed in the smell of vomit, with my jacket lying over me like a blanket, I sat up, all shaky and weird, and saw the back of Jake's head. I was lying across the backseat of his mother's Volvo.

"Where are we?"

"Almost to your house. I better help you climb up. You got pretty wasted."

"Did I fall asleep?" My voice sounded strange, a chamber-like echo. My hair and shirt were damp and cold.

"More like passed out. You barfed. Sudie helped clean you up."

"Sudie?"

"Justin's girlfriend. You met her at the bonfire. Remember?" Jake said in a sarcastic tone, he sounded angry. He parked the car in the alley.

No, I didn't remember. I was so trashed.

The cold air snapped me awake when I stepped out of the car. My shoulders shivered, and my teeth chattered. Jake helped me put my jacket on. He held his arm tight around my shoulders, and I leaned into him. My legs were unsure, my steps wobbly. All I could think about was getting up to my room and into my bed without my parents knowing.

We climbed a few rungs up the lattice; Jake was right behind me. He pushed me up, over the gutter, and onto the roof. I heard him backing himself down, two rungs at a time. His feet landed hard when he jumped to the flagstone path.

The rooftop felt sharp and gritty on my face. Frosty puffs of my breath were visible in the moonlight. I raised myself up, shook my head to clear it, and got up on all fours to look down into the backyard for Jake.

There he was, his back to me, sprinting for his car.

The crooked, shaky steps to my window were a real effort. I eased the window up and lifted my leg over the white enameled radiator, reaching down with my foot until I touched the hardwood floor.

Slow, unsteady footsteps carried me across the room and into my bathroom. *Don't stumble*, I thought. *Shhhh. Stay clear of the floorboard by the foot of the bed, the one with the loud creak.*

I stuffed the rubber stopper into the bathtub drain, turned the hot water on low, and poured some raspberry bubble bath under the spigot. Thank God my parents slept hard. Like the dead.

My mouth was desert dry. I leaned over the basin and gulped from the faucet. I stood up from the sink, wiping my hand across my mouth, and saw the total wreckage of Kara MacNeill staring back at me from the bathroom mirror. Black mascara smears ringed my eyes; my pale lips and pasty white skin had a greenish tint. My hair was all matted, a tangled mass of flattened curls that smelled like a garbage dumpster behind a fast-food restaurant.

I undressed. There were small pieces of vomit on my blouse. My jeans were zipped but unsnapped. There were a few spots of blood on the crotch of my underwear. I filled the sink and put my blouse in to soak.

When the bath was ready, I stepped into the tub and eased myself down into the hot water still drunk and unclear, aching everywhere.

The water stung me between my legs; it hurt there, hurt a lot. I put a hand over myself and closed my eyes, took in a deep breath, and let it out slowly. *Don't cry, don't cry.*

My eyes drifted up to the familiar brown stain from a leaky pipe in the corner of the ceiling. I put a glob of conditioner into my hair, smoothed it into the ends, and twisted it all up into a knot on top of my head.

I washed my face then swished the washcloth around in the bath water to rinse the makeup off. Mom got really mad if I left makeup stains on towels or washcloths.

I submerged myself in the steamy water and massaged my scalp. I let my hair down, let it fan out loose around my head in the water. *Relax*, I told myself. *You're OK.*

I'd take two aspirin when I got out and climb into my bed under the thick down comforter and flannel sheets and drop into a long, dreamless sleep.

I plucked the stopper from the drain and lay flat in the tub, watching the water drain slowly away, leaving little mounds of bubbles on my body here and there.

I dried myself and took the aspirin, pulled on a tank top and pajama pants.

Moonlight filtered in through the window onto my bed. The clear crystal beads of my grandmother's rosary sparkled against the darkness, calling me. I lifted the rosary off the bedpost, held it in my open palm, and closed my fingers around it.

Grandma, can you hear me? Help, please help.

Maybe she would come to me in a dream.

I got into bed and pulled the sheet and quilt over my head. Yes. Good—the inky blackness, the enclosed feeling. It was like hiding in a cave, alone and hibernating. Like Jake didn't exist. I'd think about this night, about Jake and me, later.

Whenever. Not now.

I pressed my grandmother's rosary to my heart and fell sleep.

The Morning After

A loud rap woke me. My bedroom door opened a crack.

"Kara? We're going to the eleven," Mom said.

When I turned my head to see her, I thought the pain might split it open. My bedside clock read 10:22 AM. I was still clutching the rosary.

"Come on, sleepyhead, get up and dressed."

It was Sunday morning. Mass.

"Can't we go to the 12:45?" I turned my face into the pillow to avoid the sunlight streaming in through my window.

"No, your Dad has to go in to the office for a few hours. Come on, get yourself ready. We're leaving in twenty minutes," Mom said, closing my door.

I rolled over, threw my covers off, and lay there staring up at the ceiling, willing myself to move a leg, an arm. Cement legs, robot arms, and a killer headache had frozen me in place. Getting up and dressing for Mass felt like an enormous task.

Somehow I forced my legs across the mattress, I hung my toes down and searched the floor for my slippers. I looped the rosary back onto my bedpost, shoved myself off the bed, and did a robotic shuffle across the hardwood floor and into my bathroom.

Ugh. A hideous, pitiful self looked back at me from the mirror, a self that had swollen, puffy eyes and pillow-marked cheeks. My tongue felt superglued to the roof of my mouth. I was thirsty, parched. OJ. I wanted a big, cold glass.

Another knock.

"Kara? Please don't make us late for Mass."

My father always sounded so damn formal. I walked to my door and pulled it open. Dad stepped back when he saw me, concern erasing his annoyed expression.

"I think I'm coming down with something. Maybe you should go without me."

"You certainly don't look well. Do you have a fever?" He touched my forehead with his fingertips. "No, no fever. How's your stomach?"

I made a face and shook my head, knowing I'd cry if I uttered one word.

"All right then, back to bed with you. Your mother will check in on you when she gets back from church." Dad walked away and headed down the stairs.

I'd pulled it off—a small miracle.

I went back into the bathroom and sat on the toilet. It burned when I peed. My blouse, still soaking in the sink, reeked of vomit. I opened my window a crack to get rid of the smell. Tears spilled down my cheeks, and I grabbed some toilet paper to wipe them away.

Another knock. The door to my room opened.

"Kara? Honey? Your dad says you aren't feeling well. What's wrong?"

"I'm in my bathroom, Mom," I called out to her. "It's probably just a twenty-four hour thing. You guys go ahead. I'll be all right."

"Oh, I'm sorry. You don't sound well. Do you have a sore throat?"

"A little."

"Take some vitamin C, OK? I'll make you some tea with honey and toast when we get back."

"Sure, sounds good."

Mom closed my bedroom door.

I listened for the click of her high heels as she walked along the wide, hardwood planks in the hallway downstairs.

The storm door slammed. My parents' conversation drifted up through my bathroom window.

"Do you think we should call the doctor?"

"Hope it's not the flu."

The wooden garage door groaned against metal tracks. The Mercedes started, backed out of the garage, and moved over the gravel driveway.

Then the house went quiet. Quiet as death.

I stared at the yellow flowers on the wallpaper as words from the Act of Contrition drifted around in my brain. *Through my fault, through my fault; through my most grievous fault.*

The wallpaper in my bathroom usually put me in a happy, sunny mood. I liked coming in here each morning at the start of my day, but everything felt different now. My mother had redecorated when I was ten and asked me to go through a thick album of wallpaper samples, to help her choose. I'd picked one with tiny yellow flowers linked together by wispy green vines, and Mom said I'd made a very sophisticated choice. Sophisticated? Oh yeah I was. A hard burst of tears shook me; my shoulders heaved, and I could barely catch my breath.

My fault. Mine. I shuddered, and tried to force those words out of my head. "NO!" I yelled, loud enough for the Moriaritys to hear me from five houses away. Shit! I clamped a hand over my mouth, hoping the whole neighborhood had gone to church.

In my room, I grabbed a cardigan from my dresser drawer, pulled it over my tank top and padded downstairs in my pajamas and pink bunny slippers. I was hyper aware of every object my skin touched: the smooth, round buttons of my cardigan, the sleek, varnished wood on the stair rail, and the tiny nubs of plaster beneath my fingertips as I drifted my hand along the wall on the way to the kitchen.

Sounds pierced the silence of the house. The creak of my steps on the stairs and the warped floorboard in the hallway, the pendulum clicking back and forth on the grandfather clock in the living room, the shuffle of my slippers on the linoleum, the familiar squeak of the refrigerator door when I yanked it open.

What? No orange juice? I almost started crying again but then saw the half-full, frosted glass pitcher sitting on the counter next to the coffee machine. I poured myself a large glass and gulped it down.

The coffee pot light was red. Mom must have forgotten to turn it off on her way out.

Coffee. Coffee might help. I poured half a mug and filled it to the brim with cream. Pouring the cream slowly, I watched the dark and light colors swirl and merge together, becoming a smooth blend of tones that turned into a soft, solid caramel shade. A flash of Mel and me as third graders in our Sunday dresses and patent leather Mary Janes ran through my head. The two of us, at the mother-daughter Communion breakfast, making coffee-milk. We'd fill three quarters of our cups with cream, then add a splash of coffee and two teaspoons of sugar.

I took my mug and sat down in the breakfast nook where I used to sit with my legs curled under me and do my homework when I was small. I remembered how cozy and safe everything seemed then, my mother cooking dinner a few steps away.

Our breakfast nook was white painted wood with wrap-around windows that made it eye-squintingly bright from the sun's light. But this day was cold and dark gray with the look of snow on the way. At least the kitchen was warm. My father must have turned the heat up before they left for Mass.

Warming my hands on the mug of coffee-milk, I curled my legs up under me and tried to reconstruct those tucked-away and safe feelings I used to have. I put two teaspoons of sugar from the ceramic bowl on the table into my coffee-milk and sipped. Ugh. Way too sweet.

I stood up to add more coffee. My hand started to shake when I picked up the pot. Then my whole arm began to tremble. I set the pot down and wrapped both arms around my body, hugging myself hard.

OK, you're OK, I tried to persuade myself, but my insides were churning and my stomach was rippling.

Down the hallway toward the powder room I ran; I flipped the toilet seat up just in time for the violent stream of OJ, coffee, and milk to spew out of me.

After my stomach was empty, I splashed water on my face and blotted it off with a beige hand towel embroidered with tiny daisies and an M for MacNeill. Folding it neatly, I carefully rehung it on the little brass rack by the sink.

The reflection of a pale ghost girl stared back at me from the powder room mirror. A ghost girl with an ashen, zombie face, and a splotchy red chest peeking out of her pale blue cardigan. I turned and walked away from her.

I climbed the stairs to my room, pulling myself hand over hand along the banister in a total fog. I got myself two aspirins from my bathroom cabinet, swallowed them with a large glass of water, and went back to bed. Drawing the covers up to my chin, I took a long, deep breath. Sleep. All I wanted was to sleep.

The ring of my phone felt like an iron spike boring into my brain. I picked it up to stop the pain. "Hello?"

"Hey, party girl, can you talk?" Mel's voice sounded so middle-of-the-day.

My night table clock read 12:22 PM. Wow. I'd slept for over an hour.

"Well? Can you? Was it the coolest of cool parties, or what? You still in love?"

"Pretty cool." My voice came out in a scratchy baritone; it sounded like gravel crunching under hiking boots. I cleared my throat.

"Whoa. Are you just getting up? I was sure by this time you'd have been dragged to Mass and back. We went to the ten."

"They went to the eleven. I stayed home."

"How'd you scam that?"

"Headache."

"Oh. As in, 'Not this Sunday, Mom, I have a headache?' That never works on my mother."

Why had I picked up? I couldn't talk to anybody, not even to Mel. Especially not Mel—I'd broken our vow. I decided right then never to tell her.

"What's up?"

It took enormous effort just to sound normal.

"When's the global studies thingy due? Did she give us an extension or what?"

"Yeah. Till next Wednesday."

"Cool. Are you almost done? I'm like halfway."

"Me too." School. Homework. Midterms. Ugh.

"Are you sure you're OK? You sound weird."

"I'm OK, just kind of tired."

"Late night, huh? I can't believe you're risking this sneak-out thing with a father like yours. It's beyond brave."

"Or just plain stupid."

Mel laughed.

"Hey, I have to go. I think they're back from Mass," I lied, needing to end the conversation.

"OK. Hey, fake a cough. Maybe you can scam a day off school. Worth a try. Later."

After Mel hung up, I missed her. My room felt empty. I wished Mel could just talk and talk and need no response from me. I wanted just to lie on my pillow with the phone to my ear and listen to her energetic, alive voice.

Alive.

My mother elbowed the door to my room open and carried in a tray of tea and toast. I'd been totally out; I never even heard her come in downstairs.

"How're you feeling, sweets?"

Worse than I'd ever felt in my life. Worse than she could ever know.

I looked at her and forced a small, wordless smile.

She set the tray down on my bed and put her hand on my forehead.

"No fever. I guess it's not the flu. Hope not."

"Mom, I'll be fine."

She busied herself doing her mom thing: She fluffed pillows behind my back, placed the tray on my lap, and poured tea from the little blue pot into my cup.

"Do you think you'll be up to going to school tomorrow? Have any quizzes or tests?"

Mel was right. Maybe I could get some time off from school. I decided I needed to.

"I'm not sure. I feel pretty bad. No, no tests."

I picked up a piece of toast and took a bite. It was perfect toast, medium brown, lots of butter.

"Thanks, Mom, this is really good." I sipped my tea and stirred some sugar in.

"Honey, is there anything you want to tell me?"

I swallowed a piece of toast wrong and coughed. They'd heard me last night. My life was over. Mom searched my face, waiting. I stalled, took another bite, and chewed.

"It's just that your dad noticed a lot of text charges on your phone and calls to and from the same number, one that neither of us recognized. He was asking about it on our way to Mass."

My father had given me the cell phone for my fifteenth birthday. He'd put me on the family plan. Yeah he did. It was just another way for him to control me, to freaking spy on me.

"Maybe the new girl, from my English class. Sophie? Remember … the one I worked on the Hesse project with? I called her a lot."

It was lame, but all I could think of in my foggy state. I sipped my tea, put on my best innocent face, and saw Jake's number scrolling across my brain.

"Oh. Sophie, yes. Well, it's probably a good idea to make those kinds of calls from home, don't you think? Your cell is more for emergencies. And there's no texting on our plan. We get charged for each one."

"OK, Mom. I'll tell my friends not to text me, and I'll watch the minutes from now on. Promise. Was Dad really mad?"

"More concerned than angry. I'll tell him it was because of a school project."

"Thanks."

Mom straightened the edge of my quilt with her hand. "Have you heard about the burial of those fetuses? Jean Moriarity was talking to me about it after Mass."

"Yeah, we did. At school."

"Such a shame." Mom shook her head and gazed out my window, lost in thought.

"Guess we can feel pretty good about helping out with the Statler campaign, huh?" she smiled, pleased with herself.

"Who else was at Mass?" I asked.

Throb. Throb. My head hurt. My mushy brain was in no mood for who-was-at-Mass conversation, but anything was better than hearing about buried fetuses or Bruce Statler.

"Oh, the usual crowd. Mrs. Connelly and her maid, the Moriarity clan, Emma asked for you, of course. Your dad dropped me home on his way to his office. You were sound asleep when I peeked in a little while ago. Dead to the world."

That sounded exactly right. Dead. Inside and out.

I pushed the tray aside and settled back into my bed, exhausted in every way.

My mother brushed her hand across my cheek. "I'll let you rest now," she said, picking up the tray. She stopped by the door of my room and wedged it open with her foot. "Call me if you need anything, OK?"

I lay there and thought yes, I did need something … something I didn't know how to ask for, something my mother probably couldn't give.

I rolled over and covered my head with a pillow. I wanted darkness. I wanted to numb out my brain. I wanted to sleep forever.

Back to School

Two loud raps on my door woke me.

"Kara? Rise and shine! I'll be downstairs."

Rise? Had to. Shine? Doubtful.

I had missed a week of school, most of it spent in bed, asleep. Mom made me go to the doctor and made him test me for mono. The test was negative, of course. Now I had to get up and get back to my life. There was an English mid-term to take.

Mom was settled in the breakfast nook with a cup of coffee, her hair shiny and smooth in the morning light.

A platter of French toast and extra crispy bacon was set on the table.

Maybe sugar would help my mood. I poured extra syrup on and added a sprinkle of powdered sugar.

Mom sipped her coffee as I dug in.

"Sleep OK?"

"Yeah. This is yum. Thanks, Mom."

I was hungrier than I thought and helped myself to more bacon and a second slice of French toast.

Studying for my English test had been a total bust; not a word from my *Siddhartha* notes had crept into the worn-out recesses of my brain. I gave up and went to bed early even though I was already overdosed on sleep.

Mom circled the rim of her coffee cup with the tip of her finger. "A boy called last night, pretty late, and wouldn't leave his name. He seemed kind of rude, really. Any idea who that was?"

My stomach lurched. *No, not yet. Don't think about him. Don't.*

"Not really," I lied. "Did Dad answer it, or did you?"

Mom took her empty cup to the sink and rinsed it. "I picked up the call. Kara, you can tell me. I went to Saint U's too, you know? We managed to meet boys." She turned from the sink and smiled. "Go out on dates even."

"If a guy calls, does that mean I want to go out with him?"

"Do you mean that you don't know who it was or that you know and you don't want to talk to him?"

"I don't want to talk to him." I took a long sip of orange juice, shocked to realize I was telling the truth. I didn't want to talk to Jake. Not now. Not ever.

"Well. I just hope, whoever he is, he's not a stalker type or anything like that."

"Jeez, Mom. Can't I have any privacy? It was probably one of the guys we sat near at the Cherry Creek game. One of them asked me my name, I shouldn't have told him. Our number is in the phone book."

My mother slotted breakfast plates and cups neatly into the dishwasher. "OK. You know your dad. He worries."

"But you said he didn't even know about the call, right? Why can't he leave me alone? I'm not a baby anymore."

So not.

My eyes burned at the thought of the party, of sneaking out, and Jake. I got up to put my plate and fork into the dishwasher.

"He only wants to keep you safe. I know your dad's strict, but he loves you very much. He really does."

"I know, I know," I said, focusing on the neatly stacked dirty dishes and silverware in front of me. But I didn't know—not deep down, not in my heart.

Any freedom I'd gotten since the seventh grade was my mother's doing. If she hadn't convinced Dad to let me go to the Cherry Creek game … an ugly thump shot through me when I thought about the game and seeing Jake for the very first time.

Closing the dishwasher door, I imagined everything I had ever felt about Jake locked inside it. Eyes closed, I pressed the button and visualized my mind being scoured clean, all memories of Jake Dodson melting away into the scalding water and soap suds of the power scrub cycle.

"Kara? Are you OK?"

I startled and crossed the kitchen to pick up my backpack.

"Yeah, I'm fine. I have to go, Mom, or I'll miss the bus." I turned and gave her a quick peck on the cheek. She hugged me to her for a moment. "Have a good day, sweets. I love you."

I hoisted my backpack and turned away from her, my eyes moist. "Me too," I said.

The day was cold and clear with a bright sun, no clouds or wind. I crossed the front lawn and began the two-block walk to the bus stop, the sun warming my face. I hated lying to my mother. It gave me a really bad feeling inside. My mother and I had created a kind of united front over the past few years. Now I was defecting, breaking rank and moving into uncharted territory, alone and without a compass. I wanted to tell her the truth, about everything. She might even understand, but if I told her about the parties, or the bonfire, any of it, and she told my father …

My bus stopped at the curb, and I thought about being grounded for eternity. It didn't sound so bad.

Thursday was a SUCH day. SUCH is an acronym for Saint Ursula's Community Help day. Depending on our moods, sometimes Mel and I referred to it as SUCK day.

Evil Elaine heard Mel say that once, and Mel got double detention plus a note detailing her "blasphemous expression" snail-mailed to her mother. That was where Mel was lucky. Her mother was in full agreement that Sister Elaine was a total nutcase. Sherry also agreed with us that Saint Ursula's should have retired her twenty years ago.

On SUCH days, we always ate lunch at eleven fifteen. It was a spaghetti and meatballs day, which was OK but not nearly as good as a hamburger day. I was first in line and let my friends cut.

Mel, Dakota, and I sat down with our lunches. I spotted Maura moving between the rows of tables with a loaded tray. I wanted her to sit somewhere else, anywhere else.

But Maura sat down right next to me.

"Well, Miss Popularity has risen from the dead," she said. "What happened? Did that ultra cool and exclusive Cherry Creek party make you sick?"

Heat rose in my face. I stared at my spaghetti; my knee was jiggling underneath the table.

"Really, how was it? Tell! Is Mr. Cool and Gorgeous still all cool and gorgeous?" Jenna asked.

The whole table hushed, waiting for my reply. Even the girls who sat at the end, the ones who weren't part of our crowd, had their ears perked.

"Oh no, let me guess. Monsieur Hottie has cooled it, am I right?" Maura used her bitchiest French accent for the monsieur part.

Mel turned on Maura. "Shut up. The party was totally awesome. Kara had the best time." Mel elbowed me, her eyebrows arched. "Amazing, wasn't it?"

"Yeah, definitely." I forced a grin.

The table of girls nodded, all of them in full-on envy.

"Older crowd, huh? Wasn't it at Rob's house? He was captain of the b-ball team last year," Dakota said. "He was an amazing player too, and cute as I remember. Right?"

"Yeah. There were mostly juniors and seniors from Cherry Creek. A few kids from DU."

I separated strands of spaghetti and moved them around on my plate in the watery tomato sauce. *You're OK*, I told myself. *Smile, like you had the best time ever.*

"Wow, college kids! Isn't that so cool?" Eyes wide, Jenna scoped out our end of the table for confirmation.

"Only if one thinks of DU as a college," Maura jeered. She twirled a big wad of spaghetti on her fork and stuffed it into her fat, nasty mouth.

The girls sitting at the other half of the table pretended to talk among themselves, but their heads were tilting in my direction, straining to overhear every detail.

"DU is all right," Mel said. "Not everyone wants to go to Yale, Maura. Or can."

"Yeah, you're such an elitist." Dakota lifted her pinky and sipped from her plastic cup. Everyone laughed.

"Yeah, I might go to DU when I get out of here, so shut up," Jenna told Maura. Then she turned to me. "So, tell. Is Jake nice or a jerk? My mother says sometimes the cutest, coolest boys are the meanest."

My mind flashed on Jake's thumb sliding beneath the waistband of my jeans, him pulling me down onto the bed, kissing me.

Stop. No, don't think about him.

"Jeez. Are you guys jealous or what?" Mel defended, elbowing me at the same time, so I would speak up for myself.

"Did he ask you to come to his next game? Or not?" Maura asked.

It was a pass-fail question.

Under the table, Mel nudged my leg with hers. Her eyes pleaded with mine: *Answer her. Come on! Don't let Maura win.*

"What do you think? Everything's all good with Jake and me," I lied, and stood up. "Anyone want anything from the salad bar?"

Tables of chatting girls surrounded me en route to the salad bar. I'd been so fixated on Jake for weeks, that I'd been oblivious of everything and everyone else. All I wanted now was the guy erased from my psyche and my world. I didn't want to be asked about him, to talk about him, or think about him, ever again.

The salad bar offered the usual mass of choices, but nothing appealed. I stalled, not wanting to return to a table full of inquiring minds that wanted to know every aspect of my exotic social life.

The bell finally rang, and everyone in the cafeteria cleared their trays and headed outside to the waiting buses.

Mel and I plopped ourselves down onto the faded black bus seats.

I sighed. "I am *so* not up for this today."

"Are you talking about doing the Hokey Pokey, changing wet Pull-ups, or reading *The Cat in the Hat* before pick-up time?" Mel asked.

Mel always made fun of SUCH days, but I think she enjoyed being around little kids as much as I did.

"I don't know. Today, I'd just rather pet dogs and cats than deal with anything that talks back."

"Samantha got the animal shelter," Dakota said.

"Oh yeah she did," Mel agreed.

"Suck Up!" we all shouted.

Mel, Dakota, and I had all wanted the animal shelter this year. But we got Head Start.

More than fifty Head Start preschoolers were running and screaming around the sandy playground as our bus entered the parking lot.

Most of these kids had no winter coats. They didn't seem to mind, though, or even notice the cold. They played on the swings and jungle gym in sweatshirts and light sweaters, unaware that they lacked warm coats, hats, and mittens.

Cole ran over to me and hugged my waist, his round eyes so dark I couldn't find the pupils.

"Hey Kara, I missed you!"

"Me too!" Reina said. She came up to hug my other side and tried to push Cole away. Reina was kind of a tomboy. She was tough but sweet in her own way.

Cole and Reina began to wrestle and push.

"Get away! Shut up!"

"You shut up, fat ass!"

"Cole, we use kind words when talking to our friends," I said.

"I hate kind words. She ain't my friend." Cole folded his arms across his chest and turned his back on Reina.

"She isn't? Reina is my friend, aren't you, Reina?"

Reina wiped a tear from her dusty cheek, leaving a little track on her smooth, caramel skin. She hugged my leg and nodded.

Cole turned his big, wet eyes away from us and stomped off into the classroom. Reina grabbed my hand, the winner.

"I hate Cole," she whispered, cupping her mouth with her tiny hand.

"No, Reina, we don't hate. Cole is our friend, too. I think he's feeling kind of sad now. We are always kind to each other. Right?"

Reina began to skip as we entered the classroom. "OK."

Dakota called Reina over to help set the table with plastic sporks and paper napkins. I saw Cole sitting alone in the block area, building tall towers and smashing them down with his little fists. I went over and gave him a hug; he relaxed into it, all smiles.

On SUCH days, we learned from the teachers at Head Start about redirecting, using "I messages," and encouraging kindness. My father could've used some time there.

At pick-up time, Cole's mother was late, as usual. I was reading *Are You My Mother?* to him when Shawna finally walked in. So far, any and all of my attempts at kindness had failed with her.

Cole ran over to her. Shawna let him hug her, but she didn't really hug back. She just kind of patted the top of his head, scanning the room with her faraway and exhausted eyes.

After a minute, Shawna looked down at her son. "Cole, where is your sweatshirt?"

Cole rushed to his cubby. Empty. He searched the other cubbies, his frantic eyes glanced my way.

Shawna put one hand on her hip. "Cole, did you lose it?"

I knelt on the floor and rifled through the lost-and-found bin.

"Can't you even keep him from losing every damn thing?" Shawna stood over me, glaring. She was always ready to accuse, to pick a fight, and it felt like she always wanted to pick one with me.

I dumped the contents of the plastic lost-and-found bin onto the rug. The sweatshirt wasn't there.

Cole's teacher, Mary Kay, came in from the playground holding a faded red sweatshirt with frayed cuffs. Cole darted over and grabbed it from her.

"You're welcome, Cole," Mary Kay said in her gentle, relaxed tone. She smiled at Shawna. "It was hanging on the jungle gym outside."

Shawna pulled the sweatshirt roughly over Cole's head.

"How was your day, Shawna?" Mary Kay asked.

"Ugly. Stupid. The usual." Even Shawna had to smile at the way she'd described her day.

"I'm sorry. Maybe you'd like to drop Cole off early one day next week, and we could talk about things for a bit?"

"Yeah, all right."

"Well, let me know tomorrow what day works for you, OK?" Mary Kay put her hand on the back of Shawna's jacket. "You two have a nice night. See you in the morning."

"OK then." Shawna blew out a deep sigh as she took Cole's hand.

Mary Kay never gave up on that kindness thing. I didn't know how she managed.

"Bye, Kara," Cole called to me, waving.

They left the classroom, and I gave Mary Kay a thumbs-up.

"It's tough raising a three-year-old on your own, especially at eighteen," Mary Kay said.

"Eighteen! Wow, I thought she was, like, twenty-five, at least."

"Shawna has had a rough time, and it shows. She needs a lot of support."

Mary Kay took a bottle of 409 and a roll of paper towels from the supply cabinet and began to wipe down the pint-sized tables and chairs.

"Thanks for helping today, Kara. I really appreciate having you girls here, and so do the children."

The Saint U's bus was pulling into the parking lot.

"OK. See you next time," I said, taking my down jacket off a hook next to the cubbies. I had kind of a strange, guilty feeling leaving Mary Kay there. I wished I was able to help her more.

Mel and Dakota were cracking up about something or other when I entered the bus. I sat down in the row behind them and scooted over next to the window. I didn't feel much like talking, or laughing. The bus driver made two more stops to pick up girls from other SUCH day programs.

The streets and neighborhoods of Denver flew past the bus window in a blur. I thought about Shawna and Cole all the way back to school. I thought about my period, too … that it was late. More than a week.

And I decided to buy a pregnancy test.

Now What?

No matter how I counted the seconds, three minutes seemed like an eternity. I stared at my bathroom wallpaper until the petals of the soft yellow flowers went out of focus, their edges morphing into a golden fuzz.

The spit of gravel in the driveway jarred me from my yellow plant-life trance. I pulled the window blind up a notch.

My father's Mercedes was hovering in front of our garage, and the double door was starting to rise from the click of his remote. He was home early.

My eyes jumped from the Mercedes to the EPT lying on the edge of my sink. A tiny cross had appeared in the result window. It was positive, *positive.*

"Shit!"

My heart thumped fast and hard, pounding up through my chest and into my ears. I stared at the little plus sign and prayed for it to change, squeezed my eyes shut and begged for it to become a minus. *Please, God. Please.* But the little plus sign was still there, mocking me. No miracle was going to happen.

Not now, not ever.

This was my second test, a different brand than the first one I'd taken when I got home from school. Both were positive.

Pregnant. I was really pregnant.

Oh my God.

The storm door opened and slammed shut, I heard the warped floorboard in the hallway off the kitchen creak under my father's heavy step.

"Kara? Come down, please, and set the table. Your dad is home," Mom called.

My father's briefcase, thick with files and depositions, slapped down on the desk in his office.

"Oh God, oh God, shit!" I said under my breath.

"Be right down," I yelled, scooping the results from the two early pregnancy tests into the empty pharmacy bag. My voice sounded shaky and strange. I hoped my parents didn't hear the weirdness like I did. I knotted the bag's top and stashed it under my bed. No, not safe. I yanked it back out and scanned my room for a better place to hide the evidence of my ruin. Nothing felt safe.

Nothing.

My eyes paused on the rosary hanging on my bedpost—the clear crystal beads, the sterling chain, and the blood-red enamel cross. My grandmother had given it to me for my Confirmation in the fifth grade. When she died three years ago, I'd hung it on my bed to keep her spirit close.

I wiped the dust from the cross with my thumb and folded my hand over the rosary. *Help me, Grandma. Help me.* What would she say if she could see me right now? I felt sick inside.

My life was wrecked—totally and forever.

"Kara … sweetie? Come on, dinner in ten."

The gargantuan pile of stuffed animals in the corner of my room, the ones my mother had saved since I'd slept in a crib and hugged them—underneath that pile was the perfect hiding place for the remains of the two positive tests.

"Coming, Mom!" I yelled.

I shoved the bag under my old teddy bears and Beanie Babies, then shut the door behind me, wishing I could lock it.

Down the stairs.

Oh God, oh God.

Through the hallway. Into the kitchen I walked, erasing all traces of panic from my face.

My father was carving a roasted chicken. A shaken and poured martini sat on the counter next to him.

"I'll be going down to Colorado Springs a lot for the Krundler case beginning next week," Dad said.

The smell of garlic and rosemary emanating from the moist, sliced chicken enveloped me. I moved around my parents to the silverware drawer on the far side of the island.

"Oh, no. You won't miss the Statler fund-raiser, will you?" My mother squeezed a half lemon over some steamed broccoli and began spooning it into a serving bowl.

"What's the date?"

"The eighteenth, six o'clock. There'll be dinner, and cocktails before."

"I've already seen him speak, when we went to the thing at the Moriaritys'. At this juncture, I think I get his agenda." My father was concentrating intensely on his carving.

Mom's face was pinched, annoyed. "I'd rather not go alone, but I guess if I have to …"

"I'll do my best to be in town for it, OK? My best." Dad sipped his martini and sighed. It was an angry, frustrated sigh.

On autopilot, I pulled silverware and red cloth napkins neatly rolled in carved teakwood rings from the drawer. *I'm pregnant. Pregnant.* My stomach gurgled, loud, like it does when I'm really nervous.

Concern wrinkled my mother's brow. "Did you eat lunch, Kara?"

"Yes, Mom. I did. We had spaghetti." My voice sounded normal, regular. I headed for the dining room, my fists full of napkins and silverware. My father carried the platter of chicken behind me.

"Maggie, grab that bottle of red on the counter, will you please?"

Wine plus a martini—my father wouldn't notice a thing. I set the table.

We all sat down, took our napkins from their rings, and laid them across our laps. Mom reached out for our hands; the three of us formed a triangle with our arms and said grace. We said "Amen" in unison.

My reflection in the silver candelabra was distorted and wide. False.

Dad forked a plump slice of chicken breast onto my plate. My stomach clenched. No food, it begged, no food! I accepted the meat anyway.

He held the serving fork above my plate. "Want a wing, too?"

"No. No thanks, Dad." Don't gag, I thought. *Breathe.*

"Jean Moriarity called today." Mom poured herself some wine. "She asked me to be on the planning committee for the fund-raiser. What do you think, Bill?"

My father helped himself to broccoli and passed the chicken to Mom.

"I guess. If you have the time … and the inclination."

There was a pause. I could feel the knot of tension between them.

"I told her I'd think about it and call her back. But, if you're going to be out of town, I—"

"I said I'd do my best, and I will," Dad said as he pulled the tooth-picked olive from his drink. He sucked on it a bit and then plopped it back into his glass. In my opinion, it was a disgusting habit.

"And how was your day, my darling daughter?"

The martini had definitely kicked in.

"OK. Nothing special."

My father could be extremely charming when he wanted to be, but that portion of his personality was usually reserved for his clients. I wished I could switch places with them—they'd get his strictness and control and I'd get the charming part.

I needed to take a breath, one regular breath.

"She got an A on her English paper. That's special."

Mom always tried to get the family conversation thing going.

"Not really." My voice went quiet and soft.

"Well, just because you always do well in English doesn't mean it's not special." My mother and father sipped red wine and shared a proud parent smile.

Pregnant. I was pregnant. How special was that? How proud would they be now? I pushed bits of food clockwise around my plate, my mind spooling out silent instructions: *Pick up fork. Chew. Smile.*

After waiting a reasonable amount of time, I pulled back my chair. "May I please be excused? I've got a ton of homework."

"You've hardly eaten a thing, Kara. Are you sure you're feeling all right?"

"Yes, Mom, I had a late snack."

"Garbage night, isn't it?" my father said as I reached the doorway. Some things he notices without fail.

I made a quick trip up to my room and pulled the plastic bag out from under the animal pile, scrunched it up, and hid it under my arm. Then I flew back down the stairs with the bag securely hidden inside my leather jacket.

I rolled the large black dumpster from the backyard into the alley behind the house and set it next to the blue recycling bin. Then, checking first to make sure the alley was clear, I sprinted the half block down to Mrs. Connolly's house.

Mrs. Connolly had lived on our street since before I was born. She had a full-time maid to take care of her now. Her maid always brought her garbage out in the early afternoon.

I opened the dumpster: two Dreyer's cartons, a Kleenex container, and some Entenmann's pastry boxes were lying on top of a cinched, black plastic bag. Mrs. C was still a sugar freak. I pulled the bag open and dumped the incriminating tests in, then scooped loose paper and junk mail envelopes over them and re-tied the bag, arranging the ice cream cartons and pastry boxes back over everything before closing the lid.

The three-quarter moon was ringed with clouds as I walked slowly back to my house. When Mrs. Connolly's husband had first died, Mom used to send me over to her house sometimes to help her. After I'd taken her garbage out or swept the back steps, she'd often invite me in for freshly baked chocolate chip cookies. They were the best cookies, with huge chunks of dark chocolate and lots of pecans. I talked about them so much that Mom had asked Mrs. Connolly for the recipe.

"Hi, Kara. Out for a walk?"

Startled, I jumped half a step to the side of the alley.

"I was just putting our garbage bin out." I said, thinking about the damning evidence I'd just gotten rid of.

Our neighbor, Jean Moriarity, was walking toward me with her Dalmatian on a leash.

"How's school going this year?" she asked.

"Hi, um, school's good." I mumbled, in no mood for a neighborly chat.

"Emma just loves it, loves it. She said she saw your name on the honor roll list in the lobby at school. That's great.... Sparky! Get down!"

I hated the Moriarity's dog. Sparky was a biter. He'd chased Mel and me up a tree once. We were in third grade, playing tag in my front yard. He tried to bite my mother's hand off when she came out to shoo him away.

"Thanks."

"Emma's thinking of going out for track ... Sparky, NO!"

Sparky bared his teeth at me and strained against the leash. Mrs. Moriarity yanked on his choke collar, and the dog stood still. They should muzzle him, I thought. Better yet, they should put the monster to sleep.

"How did you enjoy JV track, Kara?"

Emma Moriarity went to Saint Ursula's, too. She always waved when she saw me and tried to talk to me at the bus stop. What a pain. She was only twelve, a seventh-grade baby. I felt way older than that now. Decades.

"Cross-country, not track. It was OK. I'd better get going though, Mrs. Moriarity. I've got loads of homework." I gave a wave and walked on.

"Tell your mother I said to call me, OK? And Kara? Thank you for helping us send out that mailer for the Statler campaign. I think all our hard work is going to pay off."

"Sure," I answered in my good-girl voice, wishing I hadn't let my mother guilt me into helping.

"Have a nice night, dear."

Nice. Oh yeah. Only the worst night of my entire life. No, if I really let myself think about it, the second worst.

I stopped in front of my garage and listened to the sounds of my neighborhood. Rubber dumpster wheels bouncing over ruts and gravel, were being pushed along driveways and footpaths to the alley. Neighbors laughed and called out to each other in the still night air, the same neighbors I'd always known from the same older wood and brick homes. Dogs barked. A honking horn alerted everyone that a car was backing into the alley.

The sounds that used to feel safe, comforting, and familiar, the sounds from my used-to-be regular, normal life now felt strange and far away, like I was out of sync and didn't belong anymore.

My heart hurt. I didn't remember ever feeling so bad, so all on my own, so helpless.

I couldn't run in to my mother this time and say, "I skinned my knee" or "So-and-so hurt my feelings," and have a Band-Aid put on or get a kiss from her to make it all better.

No one, nothing, could make this better.

Telling Jake

Cheesman Park was cold and brown. Lifeless. The naked tree branches, coated with ice, were unbending and brittle. The park was only asleep for the winter but appeared so completely dead it seemed impossible that it could ever come alive again. Like me.

As I walked along the bike path, my mind spun out in a million directions.

What would Jake say ... what if he didn't believe me?

My plan was to call Jake's cell number from a phone booth. After being one of the only kids in my class without a cell phone, now I was afraid to use the one I had. My father would check the bill, find Jake's number, and grill me. My cell phone had turned into a leash, another way for my father to keep a constant check on me.

I saw a phone booth across the park near the dried-up water fountain by the gazebo and headed for it, walking along the jogging path. Images from the party flooded my head. Hot tears turned cold on my cheeks. There were no sobs, no sound at all, just tears streaming down my face faster than I could wipe them away.

At first, I was embarrassed but then I realized there wasn't a soul in the park to see me cry. There was no one to hear me, no one to see me.

No one to help me.

A few steps before reaching the phone booth, I slapped myself down hard on a slatted wood bench. "You stupid, stupid girl!" I scolded, out loud.

I didn't care what happened to me then. Getting hit by a car sounded good. A truck would be even better. I wanted never to have to deal with this, never to tell a single soul. Never to have to decide.

There was comfort in the silence of the empty park. The rough, gray wood of the bench had once been painted a deep green, but only a few flecks of color remained here and there. The iron legs had long ago rusted to a dark brown.

It was cold, maybe twenty degrees, or lower with the wind chill. My clenched hand was red and raw against the worn wood of the bench, and my forehead ached from the icy air. My gloveless hand didn't hurt much because I was numb; an all-over numb, inside and out.

I'd rushed out without gloves or a hat to call Jake and tell him the awful truth—a word I didn't even want to think about, much less say aloud.

Pregnant.

I needed a do-over. "Do-over!" I yelled across the vacant park.

In elementary school, Mel and I used to give each other do-overs in jump rope and dodge ball. I wanted one now.

I shoved my hands deep into the pockets of my ski jacket and stared at the sun-beaten bench for a long moment, at the round, wet mark next to my thigh where my fist had melted the frost. What if I fell asleep? I wondered how long it would take for me to freeze to death and laughed out loud at the thought of being found on some random bench in Cheesman Park, a popsicle girl, my body a total frost of ice.

My breath moved out of me in quick, white puffs, and I started to laugh, really laugh. Maybe I was going crazy. I didn't care; it felt great to laugh. To breathe, soul-deep, great gulps of cold air.

I leaned against the hard slats of the bench, suddenly composed, almost ready to make the call to Jake.

But the thought of talking to him, actually telling him, twisted my stomach into a granny knot, the kind we'd learned in Girl Scouts, the kind that's hard to undo. I knew just what he'd say. He'd say that I was wrong, that you couldn't get pregnant from doing it once.

Well, guess what? You could.

My frozen fingers shoved coins into the slots of the pay phone and dialed his cell.

"Hello?" Jake's voice sounded happy and up.

"Jake? It's Kara."

"Hey. What's up?" His voice became icier than the wind in my hair.

"I'm in the park."

"Jesus. What for? It's freezing out."

"I'm pregnant."

There. Done.

There was total silence on the other end of the line. The tears were flowing again; I sniffed them back, not caring if Jake heard me.

"No way. Shit, are you sure? You can't be."

"I took a test. Two tests. I am."

"I'll be there in ten minutes," Jake said, and his end of the line went dead.

I jumped up and down, slapping my hands together hard to warm my body like I'd learned to do in a ski class when I was seven. Maybe I really would freeze.

My sneakers crunched the wintry soil and cinders as I moved my legs, walking fast along the jogging path. I wanted to move away from myself, away from thoughts of Jake, away from everything.

Two years of running cross-country kicked in. Walking became jogging, jogging became running, and then I ran, full out, picking up my pace. Running felt good, really good. The icy wind stung my face, but my body warmed. Gaining speed, I raced into the wind. Head on and fast. So fast the trees became a blur. Alive, I felt alive. I ran lap after lap until I lost count.

"Kara, Kara!"

Bounding, long-legged strides were following mine. Faster, faster, gaining on me. Jake was in the park.

Warm bursts of white mist escaped my mouth. One more lap, I needed just one. But I couldn't go on. I stopped and fell to my knees, exhausted and sobbing.

Jake crouched beside me and put his hand on my shoulder. "Don't cry. Jesus. Stop," he said and pulled me up. We walked silently along the jogging path and out of the park.

We drove to a diner on the south side of town. After parking the car, Jake leaned across my lap to open my door. There was his body, lying across mine the same way he had on the night of the bonfire.

My stomach clenched. I didn't want Jake's body anywhere near mine, didn't want his chest touching my jeans, my lap. I cringed and held my arms up, away from him. I wanted him off of me. *OFF!*

Jake flung my door open and moved back onto the driver's side then opened his own door and got out. "Don't just sit there. Jeez," he said.

I trailed after him into the diner.

Two truckers sat on counter stools eating fried eggs and beans. They had steamy tortillas dripping with butter folded in their hands. Neither of them noticed us walk by and take a booth. This diner, the waitress, the truckers, and Jake, all of it, seemed strange and totally unfamiliar.

I'd never been to the diner, never even passed by the place in a car, but that was a good thing. Anonymity. For days I'd felt as if I had a neon sign flashing on my forehead that read: "Pregnant. This girl is pregnant."

The waitress cruised over to our table, all smiley and happy. She had a streak of green eye shadow over each eye and glittery rouge leaking into the lines of her crinkly cheeks. Jake ordered two hot cocoas.

I tucked one foot under myself and tapped the other softly against the underside of the booth. Jake was drumming his index finger on the table, his eyes on the truckers.

On the other side of the greasy, fingerprint-smeared window, snow began to fall. Tiny fingers, three-year-old sized, had left their mark on the thick glass, partially obstructing my view. A crude smiley face had been drawn with small handprints on either side. I thought about Cole, Mary Kay, and Head Start afternoons.

My hands were tingly; they stung. I flexed my fingers.

"Come on, Kara. It's gonna be OK." Jake grabbed my hand.

I pulled away and focused my gaze outside, on the falling snow.

"Kara? You hear me?"

I met his eyes. "Yeah, and you're wrong; it's not going to be okay. There's no good way out of this. Not for me anyway." My voice sounded sharp and unfamiliar, a world away from the self I used to be. I was living a split-in-two life: before Jake, and after.

"B. W. + S. D." Sweethearts' initials were carved into the gray Formica tabletop in front of me; a speck of dried egg yolk formed an accent above the W.

I adjusted my sitting position. The red leatherette seat beneath me was cracked and dry.

"Mistakes happen," Jake continued. "No friggin' way you're going to have it. Are you even sure it's mine?"

That stung me like a slap.

"This is more than a mistake," I said. "And yeah, most definitely yours."

"Shit, weren't you even on the Pill or anything? All girls are." Jake seemed more mad at me than upset with himself. His beautiful eyes looked mean and hard.

"I wasn't. You never bothered to ask."

"I got a girl pregnant before, and she didn't make any big deal out of it. No hassles. She did the right thing."

"And what was that?"

"Got rid of it, of course. She was all cool about it, too. Do you think you're going to wreck my life because of some random hookup?"

Wreck your *life? Random hookup?* My mind reeled.

"Mine already feels pretty wrecked, thanks."

For a few seconds I made believe that I was in the middle of a nightmare, pretended that I could wake up never having met this guy. Wishing, wishing, wishing I could make him, and every moment I'd spent with him, disappear.

Jake had the same redness in his cheeks and ears that my father got when he was really frustrated, like a defective pressure cooker ready to blow.

"Here you go, extra whipped cream!" the waitress said, setting our cocoas down and slapping some spoons and white paper napkins on the Formica with a big smile, as if she could pump some fun into our harsh conversation with a whipped cream bonus.

"Thanks, ma'am." Jake grinned, oozing fake charm all over her.

"You got yourself a cutie, hon," she said with a wink.

My eyes went flat. I didn't have anything.

The waitress smiled anyway and moved across the diner like the Energizer Bunny, pouring refills for the truckers and other customers who held out their white enamel mugs to her.

"Hey," Jake said, forcing my gaze back to his rigid face. "Let me tell you what, OK? I've got me a mondo b-ball career happening, in case you forgot, and a full scholarship to Notre Dame in the works. I'm gonna go pro someday, and I'm not blowing that for anything. Or anyone. You got that?"

Zero reaction from my side of the booth. I spooned whipped cream into my mouth from the top of my cocoa. A small glob dropped onto the table next to my mug.

"You're a nice girl, sure, and we went out a few times. But I've gone out with lots of girls. You went upstairs with me. You said you wanted to. Don't act all innocent."

My spoon clattered to the table. I gripped its grimy top with both hands and leaned toward Jake. "I *am* all innocent! I've never had a boyfriend, never even gone to a coed party before. Never kissed anyone! You got *that*?"

Jake's eyes rolled. He held in a chuckle. "Oh, shit, don't tell me. You're a virgin?"

"Not anymore." A sob throttled in my throat, and I forced it back.

Jake swiveled in his seat, looking to see if anyone was close enough to hear, and then turned back to me. "Chill, OK? Come on. Listen, have you told anyone?" His voice softened. He was trying to soothe me, to shut me up.

"No. No one."

Relief washed over Jake's stupid face. Was he even attractive to me now?

I felt so messed up—in my body, in my mind, in my whole life. I thought—I really, truly thought—that if Jake would only say that he loved me, that he would no matter what I decided to do, I'd somehow feel better. Insane? Sure, and I knew it, but I still wanted to hear those words. I wanted Jake to say that he'd loved me that night, that he'd even marry me if I wanted him to, that he would support me in having his baby.

Marrying Jake would be the worst choice ever. I knew that. No possible doubt. But I just really wanted to hear him say, "I love you." Once.

Jake was a silent lump. He was a tall, hulking idiot staring out the window at the snowstorm. I fingered tiny circles in the small pool of melted whipped cream and chipped at the hardened egg yolk with my thumbnail.

"Nothing's wrecked. Get an abortion." Jake's voice was soaked with anger.

I looked evenly at him. "Right. I'm fifteen; I can't even get birth control without my parents' permission."

Jake leaned closer and clenched his teeth. "Well, get your friggin' parents' permission then." It was a thick whisper, sandpaper rough.

Outside, the snow was falling harder; close to three inches already covered the ground. The cars in the parking lot had turned into white, rounded mounds.

My face felt hot, and my eyes were wet. I squeezed them shut against a giant tear, but it slid down my cheek anyway. Flicking it away like a pesky fly, I realized how mad I was, at Jake, at the world, at everything.

"Easy for you to say. So easy, Jake. You won't be getting an abortion or having to have a baby! No, everything's on me. All of it."

Jake leaned back and stifled a yawn. His eyes rose up to the water-marked asbestos tile ceiling. "Get that abortion pill then. RU-whatever, from France or Europe, wherever."

I was silent, staring at him.

Jake took my hands and put on a sweet-talk smile. "It's not that hard, you know. Girls deal with this stuff all the time. They figure it out."

I yanked my hands away from him and wrapped them firmly around my mug. *Oh yeah,* I thought. *So easy. For you, just sitting by, letting someone else take care of the dirty work, letting someone else be your dirty work. Right. Just take care of this little problem for me and get out of my life.*

Jake wanted an abortion. Any way he could make me have one. He wanted it for himself.

I blew across the top of the cocoa and sipped. It was real milk, not a powdered cocoa mix. I wiped a trace of whipped cream from my lower lip and looked at Jake with nothing on my face. Nothing.

The waitress's head bobbed up over the back of our booth, smack into the middle of our intensity.

"Sure y'all don't want some pie? We got chocolate pecan today, and it's real good!" In her cheery, bright-eyed mode, she had no clue.

Jake kept his back to her and discharged a loud, blunt no. Zero fake charm. The waitress scooted away, afraid of blowing her tip.

"You're just all weird about this because you're Catholic. All that crap they teach you at Saint Ursula's has messed up your head."

Hundreds of buried fetuses, the prayer Sister Elaine made us say, Father Miller's sermons, all of that was burning through my mind. I wanted to punch Jake's ignorant, selfish face.

"Shut up! OK? Shut your big, fat mouth!" The words shot out of me, sudden and sure. I eased myself back against the booth, exhausted, an emotional flat line. Breathe, I told myself, *breathe*. Behind me, the truckers' forks scraped against their white diner plates.

Jake gave a miniscule not-my-problem shrug. He'd given me all the brilliant advice he had. We turned our wordless gazes out the fingerprinted window. Two sets of vacant eyes fixed on the falling snow.

After a few minutes, Jake uncoiled his long body from the booth and threw five dollars down. "Come on. Let's go."

The snow fell harder, and the wind was intense. Jake had to drive slowly and carefully, but I sensed his urgency, felt him wishing he could go faster so he could get rid of me, get me the hell out of his car, and forever out of his life.

Wrapped in the thickening silence, I acted totally calm, as if everything was just perfect. Jake kept his eyes on the road and his thoughts to himself, and so did I, determined not to cry. I'd never known the kind of fear I was feeling, the total, all-over dread; I had no words for it.

We pulled up in front of my house, and I opened the car door. Fat snowflakes began to collect on the sleeve of my down jacket.

"I'll call you," Jake said. He stared straight ahead, his jaw slumped against the steering wheel.

"OK," I said, but my guts were screaming: *Liar*. I put one leg out of the car and hesitated, hoping Jake would touch my arm or try to turn me back toward him. I wanted him to stop me. But he never moved or said one word.

I stepped out and slammed my door. Jake's snow tires carved neat, black lines into the fresh snow as he drove away. My eyes followed his car until it was swallowed up by the whiteout of the storm.

At the front door, I shook layers of fresh snowflakes from my hair and shoulders and straightened my shoulders, preparing to enter the house.

My father was sitting in the cane-backed rocker in the living room, his eye on his watch. I hoped my bloodshot eyes gave me an overachieving, mentally exhausted look, the look of a daughter who'd spent a study-filled afternoon in a dimly lit library carrel.

"Hey Dad, sorry I'm late. I was at the library. I had so much research to do for my English paper. I needed to use some archive books, the ones they don't lend out."

"I know what archive means. English class is something that your mother and I need to talk to you about," my father replied.

"You mean my paper?"

"No. An interim report we received from your English teacher."

Could anything else go wrong? My heart pounded; my already nervous state amped. My father stood and followed me down the hallway to the kitchen.

"Hi, Mom."

She was standing at the island, tossing a spinach salad in a clear glass bowl. "Hi, honey. Why didn't you take your cell? We called and called."

"I forgot it. Sorry. It's on the charger, in my room."

"Irresponsible," Dad said, edgy.

"We were worried. Please bring the napkins and the water pitcher," Mom said.

"Very irresponsible," Dad muttered, taking the pitcher of water before I got to it.

I grabbed the napkins and followed them into the dining room. We sat down, silently unfolded our napkins onto our laps, and said grace. Remains of the hot cocoa soured in my throat. There was a strong possibility that I'd be sick before taking one bite of my dinner.

My mother and father exchanged a concerned-parent glance and pounced.

"So, the basic gist of Sister Nivard's note is that your grades are headed south." The furrow in my father's brow grew a half-inch deeper. "According to the interim report, it won't be long until your grade in English is a D."

A no-win situation was headed my way.

"She's only concerned because the quality of your work has slipped so much in just the last month. She's afraid you may not qualify for AP English senior year." Mom didn't really seem angry.

But my father did. "Then there's the C minus on your midterm. Unacceptable, Kara, completely unacceptable."

Heat spread through my chest and up into my neck. My eyes filled. "Quit attacking me, both of you! I'm no slacker, and I never have been." I stood up, threw my napkin down on the table, and ran out of the room.

"Kara! Come back here. Now!" my father roared.

And I completely ignored him.

Stomp, stomp, stomp. Down the hallway, up the stairs, I moved toward my room like I was possessed, like another girl had taken over my body and was controlling my every move.

"Kara … honey? Can we just talk about this?"

I slammed the door on my mother's voice, threw myself across my bed, and wrapped my arms tightly around myself. I began to rock back and forth. I was alone in this, all alone.

Mom opened my door and saw me rocking and crying, totally losing it. She came over and sat down next to me..

"Sweetie, what's wrong? We're concerned; that's all. English has always been your best subject. You'll bring your grade up."

My father stayed in the doorway. "You just made the honor roll, for heaven's sake. Can't you understand why we'd be upset? This came at us out of nowhere."

My father leaned against the doorjamb. The anger had evaporated from his voice. I cried harder, unable to stop myself.

Mom was smoothing my hair with her hand. She placed a tissue from the box on my nightstand over my clenched fist. "Kara, honey. Don't."

My father walked into the room and stood by the foot of my bed. "Come on, Kara. Take control of yourself. You're a good student, and you'll work this out. Your mother and I have every confidence in you." His voice sounded ultra calm.

Mom leaned over and put her arms around my face-down body.

"Of course we do. You'll handle this. Come on down now and eat your dinner."

I'd freaked them out, freaked us all out. I sat up, wiping at my eyes with the tissue. "I'm not hungry. I don't want dinner."

"Well, come and sit with us then. We won't talk further about the interim report," Dad offered.

"Promise," Mom added.

They'd turned into two naughty children, swearing to be good to get out of trouble. I took a low, deep breath. "Give me a minute."

They left my room, afraid to say more.

In my bathroom, I covered my face with a cool, damp cloth. The total crash-and-burn state of my life flashed before me.

I had to go down there and act like there was nothing wrong in my world with the exception of a few bad grades. A shiver went through me, and my hands and feet tingled.

"Kara?" Mom's voice floated up from the foot of the stairs. "Sweetie?"

"I'll be right down." I called.

How could I even look at them? I could. I had to. I wrung out the facecloth, laid it on the edge of the sink, and pointed a finger at my image in the bathroom mirror.

"Get a grip," I said, and headed downstairs.

Who's the Blonde?

The frigid air burned into my lungs as I jogged up Colfax Avenue.

Jake's game was at East High. I'd told my mother I had to meet Mel a half hour before the game to get good seats. That was partially true, at least. Mel was meeting me, and we'd be together, but I needed to see Jake first, to find him out front before the game so we could talk and figure out what to do.

Jake was standing on the gray stone steps in front of the school with the usual mob of fans surrounding him. I waved, but his eyes glossed over me like he didn't know me, as if I was invisible.

Maybe he didn't see me? I moved to the left of a horde of kids, a few steps above him, and waved again. No, he saw me. Jake definitely saw me. And turned away.

Then I saw her: tall, ash blond, the flirty cheerleader from Dell's party and the bonfire. The same girl who'd watched me scarf down Jell-O shots at Rob's party.

Jake put his hand on her shoulder, and she leaned into him, her chin against his chest, smiling up into his face. Jake glided his hand over her pale hair, took her hand and smiled his big smile. He twined his fingers through hers as they climbed the steps together. A herd of Jake worshippers followed behind the happy couple.

My hand clamped down on my thudding heart. Kids ran past me, bumped into me, and almost knocked me over. I was rigid and voiceless, standing statue-like on the cold, gray steps. A different pack of Jake addicts flew by me, up the steps, two at a time. Some of them were Cherry Creek girls I recognized from the parties and the bonfire. They glanced away from me, the see-through girl with the brittle, glass heart.

I gulped freezing air and coughed, then spun around and ran up the steps to the gym to stand in the ticket line, gasping in the warm, moist air with my eyes rooted to the sneaker-scuffed floor.

Soon after, Mel showed up with Dakota. She tapped me on the shoulder and they cut in. Mel hadn't told me she was bringing Dakota, but I couldn't be jealous after the way I'd ignored her. Dakota and Mel had gotten a lot tighter since Jake. No doubt.

Despite mobbed bleachers, Mel, Dakota, and I crammed ourselves into decent seats as the players were introduced.

"Captain for Cherry Creek, Jake Dodson, number twenty-one!" Jake jogged out onto the court. The Cherry Creek side erupted in hoots, screams, and foot stomping. "Jake, Jake, Jake!!"

My heart was pounding.

Mel nudged me. "Got to admit, he's a fairly fine specimen." She shouted and clapped for him, a peace offering of sorts. Dakota grinned at me, put two fingers into her mouth, and whistled.

The long row of cheerleaders jumped up and down in short, pleated skirts and Cherry Creek tops, waving pom-poms and shrieking cheers. My eyes stopped on the busty blond girl. Jake's girl. Front and center. She was a captain, too.

The buzzer sounded. Jake sank a shot from the foul line in the first few seconds of the game.

The crowd broke into a frenzy.

"Not bad at basketball either!" Mel yelled.

Sadness welled up, snatching my breath away. I held my hand over my stomach. "Ladies room!" I shouted in Mel's direction and cut my way through the crowd to the steps in the middle of the bleachers.

Dabbing a wet paper towel under my eyes, I tried to blot the tears, prevent swelling, and keep my mascara from running all at the same time.

Mel walked in and headed for a stall. "Dakota's saving our seats," she called over her shoulder. Then she saw my face and stopped. "Hey, what's up?"

I shook my head, unable to speak, and yanked another paper towel from the dispenser with a shaky hand.

"Did you and Jake have a fight? What's wrong? Tell me."

"Not exactly, I mean, he, I don't know, it's like …" My mouth wasn't working.

"Like?" Mel prompted.

"Like … I'm pregnant."

Mel's mouth fell open, and her eyes got huge. "Oh. My. God! No way! I mean, I had no idea you guys were even … Hey, sometimes those early pregnancy tests are wrong. Are you positive, I mean, sure?"

We both ignored her unintentional pun.

"I took two, different brands. Both were positive, and my period's way late."

Mel scowled. "Does Jake know?"

"Yeah he does. He said to get an abortion, ASAP. Believe me, it's no biggie for him."

"Oh, wow. What about your parents?"

"Of course not! If they find out, I'm dead. They don't even know I snuck out with him. Mel, don't say a word. Don't tell anyone, not Dakota, anyone. Promise."

"Don't worry," Mel said. "I'd never."

We stood in the surround sound of echoing screams and the buzzing scoreboard.

"Did jerk-face have anything else to say? Sorry, but like, ugh."

"No. To him, this is all *my* problem."

"Bullshit!"

"I don't know what to do, Mel. I'm so scared."

"You've gotta talk to someone—your mom or a counselor. Someone. Dakota's mother is a counselor. Maybe my mom? She'll know what to do."

"Shooting myself sounds better. I'm not telling *anyone*. I shouldn't have told you!"

That sounded harsh even though I didn't mean it to. Mel reached out to put a hand on my shoulder, but I jerked away from her touch. Kindness from anybody would generate a blubber-fest, a monsoon.

"Don't. I wish I were dead," I whispered.

"No, Kara. Never say that. Never."

Footsteps and echoing laughter approached from outside the bathroom. A group of talking, teasing girls was headed our way through the cinder-block hallway.

Mel pushed me into a stall, closed the door behind us, and put a finger to her lips.

We heard the bathroom door swing wide. The girls hurried in. I stifled my misery and peeked through the crack in the stall door.

They were Cherry Creek juniors and seniors, part of Jake's crowd. They pulled makeup and hairbrushes out of their purses and continued talking.

"Did you see him with Sedona outside before the game? They're sooo cute together! Dell told me Jake's totally hot for her."

"Yeah he is. That Saint Ursula's chick is so over."

"She was *so* not cool enough for Jake."

"No way."

"I heard she barfed all over him at Rob's party."

"Oh yeah she did. Sudie had to clean her up. Yuck. For sure the girl can't hold her Jell-O shots."

They were totally dissing me.

Mel was watching through the other crack in the door. I felt so exposed. I grabbed the door handle of the stall. I wanted to open it and scream at them, to pull their hair out by its dark roots, and flip them off. Mel put her hand over mine, and her finger went to her lips again. She mouthed, "Don't," and shook her head.

Freshly glossed and primped, the girls drifted out of the bathroom.

We waited for the close of the girls' room door and exited the stall.

My head was down, shoulders slumped. I didn't know what to say but Mel didn't even ask me about their gossip.

"Do you know how far along you are?" she asked.

"A couple of weeks. Jake hasn't called or anything since I told him. I saw him outside with that girl, one of the cheerleaders, Sedona."

"Ugh."

"The captain."

"Double ugh!" Mel sneered.

I flashed on Jake touching her hair.

"The little shit," Mel said, like she was reading my thoughts.

"No. A mondo one." We shared a sad smile at my stupid joke.

"We're gonna deal with this, OK? Somehow. We are." Mel hugged me.

The crowd in the gym screamed and shouted, louder and louder.

"JAKE, JAKE, JAKE!!" Another score for Jake.

My eyes burned, and something in me let go. I broke down and wept on Mel's shoulder.

"That son of a bitch," Mel said.

Murderer?

My major challenge every day became going to school and trying to act normal. Drifting through the library stacks during study hall, I heard hushed voices and stifled giggles behind a wall of books.

"Guess who I saw holding some knock-out blonde's hand at the Cherry Creek Mall on Saturday."

"Who?"

"Jake the jock."

"No way!"

"Way. He was all over her."

"He's a scammer. I knew it."

"Who didn't? Except Kara."

I pushed some books aside and through the space created between the black metal shelves, I saw Maura and Jenna sharing wicked grins.

They turned and saw me.

"Shit," Maura hissed, caught in her own bitchiness.

I rushed to the end of the aisle, rounded the bend, and took a few steps toward them, putting myself right in their nasty faces. I wanted to watch Maura squirm, up close and personal.

"I'm sorry," Jenna said, her eyes locked on her uniform shoes.

"Me too," Maura added. Her eyes studied the ceiling.

"Yeah, right," I said.

"No, really. What a dork. She wasn't much," Maura offered.

Jenna nodded in agreement. "Yeah. She really was kind of slutty."

"Nice try, you weren't even there," I said. Sedona's image snapped into my head. My right eye twitched. *Don't cry*, I thought, *don't. Don't let Maura know.*

"Whatever. He's a total jerk," I told Jenna. "Your mother was so right."

Jenna blanked and then said, "Oh, you mean about the good-looking ones?"

"Yeah, I guess." I lifted my shoulders in a shrug.

A round stump of a woman in a black habit appeared at the end of the stacks, glaring at us. Her bushy eyebrows were set in sharp forward slashes above black bullet eyes. Sister Square Root, Mel called her, the library nun. Holding a rigid finger to pale, scrawny lips, Square Root swished down the aisle toward Maura, Jenna, and me. Her beady eyes seared into us, and her long, dark robes rustled against her stubby, black-stockinged legs.

"You are disturbing people who are trying to do their work. Be seated and hush, or you will all get a detention!" She pointed to the tables in the center of the library, tables of "good girls" who were studying quietly.

"Sorry, Sister," we muttered in unison and filed silently behind her down the narrow aisle to an empty table. In library-quiet mode, we sat down, and opened our books. We pulled pens and note-books from our backpacks.

Sister Square Root threw us a final watch-it look and stepped behind the check-out desk. Maura and Jenna shared a smirk.

Now everyone would find out that Jake had dumped me. Not just our class, but the entire student body. Maura would make sure of it. Damn her. I flipped the pages of my open book, seeing nothing, unable to read, to think, or to care.

By the middle of Spanish, my stomach was doing flip-flops. I raised my hand and asked for a lavatory pass. Mel's worried eyes connected with mine as I rushed past her desk and out of the room.

After a few gulps of tepid water from the fountain, I leaned my forehead against the cool green cinder-block wall for a long minute. My mind wouldn't stop spinning. *Don't panic*, I told myself, *you'll be OK.*

In the half-wall of mirror above the long row of white sinks stood a teary-eyed girl, a whopper of a pimple sprouting on her chin. I put the flat of my palm against the bathroom mirror to cover my face. I didn't want to look at me. There was the reflection of the crucifix from the bathroom wall behind me right next to my hand. Jesus, watching me. Judging me.

"Murderer," I whispered. Was that what my parents would call me if they knew what I was thinking about? Sister Elaine and Father Miller would. No doubt.

Would the baby have Jake's eyes? Was it a real baby now—a life, like my parents and the Church believed, from the moment of conception? Or was it only a bunch of cells, with no brain, no lungs, no way to sustain life on its own, like Mel said.

Cells. Multiplying cells inside my body with a design of their own. Like a cancer, taking me over and using me as a host. I dropped my hand and stared at my image in the mirror.

"No. You're not. Not a murderer," I whispered.

It felt like the real victim was me—my soul.

I touched my pimple and frowned. I shook my head, forcing stray thoughts about Jake from my brain. The key, I decided, was not to care. Not about how I looked or about what Sister Elaine, Father Miller, or my parents would do if they found out. Most of all, I didn't want to care about Jake, what he thought, or whether he knew what I decided to do—or not do.

I put fresh gloss on my lips and covered my fear with a smile. I had to go back to class and get through another day.

After-School Snack

Mel and I got off the bus at her stop and walked to her house like we had so many times. Since we'd first become friends in the second grade, we'd had a zillion sleepovers, after-school snacks, and exam crams at Mel's. It was easy to be at Mel's house. I felt free there because I wasn't being watched and worried about every second.

It was weird; my father hadn't always been so strict, or mean. We'd had good times when I was small. Lots of them. And fun too, times when I felt really connected to him, like I could talk to him about anything. As if he could fix any problem I'd ever have. But by the end of middle school, everything changed. My father became my biggest problem, my jailer, and I still hadn't figured out why.

For the two-block walk, I imagined that Mel and I were on our way to hang out, scarf down a bag of chips with salsa and guacamole, watch a movie, and do homework. The usual.

We threw our backpacks on the floor by the back door in Mel's kitchen.

A clear picture of Mel's father jumped into my mind. I saw him standing at the stove, cracking jokes, and making cinnamon apple crêpes with crème fraiche for Mel and me on a Saturday morning after I'd spent the night. I felt double guilty about breaking the vow I'd made with Mel.

Mel was scoping out the refrigerator.

"You hungry?" she asked.

"No, I still feel kind of nauseous."

Stacks of takeout and Tupperware containers lined the shelves of their Sub-Zero. Mel's dad was everywhere in the kitchen. I was sure Mel felt it, too, but she never talked about it. Her father had been the best cook, but sadly, Mel's mother's culinary genius included a drawer of takeout menus and a freezer full of restaurant leftovers.

"Mind if I eat?"

I shook my head.

Mel took a log of goat cheese and a bottle of cranberry juice out of the fridge. She pulled a box of crackers and a plate from the pantry. Grabbing a knife, she spread lumps of cheese evenly over each wheat cracker on the plate. The tiniest whiff of goat cheese nearing my nostrils made me feel like I was going to barf. I held my breath and moved to the opposite end of the island.

"Mel?"

"Yeah?"

"I'm sorry."

Mel looked up from her carefully cheesed cracker. "Don't blame yourself. Jeez."

"No, I mean …"

Mel waited, holding another cracker, a slab of goat cheese poised for spreading on her knife.

"Our vow, you know? I broke it."

Mel put the cracker and knife down. She took a sip of cranberry juice. "I sort of knew that. Like, when the Cherry Creek girls were dissing you? Jell-O shots and barfing all over yourself was kind of a tip-off."

"Oh. Right. So, you're not mad?"

"No. Somewhat disappointed, but, y' know, whatever. I sort of figured, big jock, big parties, big kegs … just saying 'no' probably didn't cut it. I guess you couldn't really, not without …"

"Yeah," I interrupted, not wanting to hear any excuses for my stupid, stupid mess-up. "But still, we promised. Believe me, I wish I hadn't."

"Well, don't make yourself all crazy. At the moment, you've got a bigger problem to deal with. But … can I ask you something? Like, why didn't you use birth control … isn't Jake eighteen? Or if somehow that messed up, for like five days or so afterwards, Plan B can prevent…"

We heard the storm door burst open. Mel's eyes rose up to the shiny copper pots hanging above our heads. I was relieved we were interrupted before I had to answer her questions.

"Don't worry; I'll get rid of him," she said.

Mel's little brother, Troy, blustered in, dragging his loaded backpack behind him. He tossed it down on the floor next to ours and pulled a stool up next to Mel.

"Hey dudes, wassup?"

I squashed a laugh. Troy was not exactly ghetto with his dirty blond skater cut and glass blue eyes. He was too cute. For a ten-year-old brother, I thought, he wasn't half bad, but Mel disagreed. She always said she'd trade only-child status with me any day.

"Homework, for you," Mel said.

"I don't have any."

"Liar. You have that social studies project. Is that finished?"

He smirked. Mel had him. Troy's smirk was almost as good as Mel's sneer.

"It's pretty done. What do you care?"

Troy reached for one of Mel's perfectly cheesed crackers, but she yanked the plate out of his reach. "You have a math lesson too, right? Your teacher assigns one every night. Don't BS me."

Troy shrugged and gave her a reluctant nod.

"Troy, I'm in charge until Mom gets home from work, and you know it."

"I get to have a snack first."

Mel grabbed a half-empty bag of cheese doodles from the pantry and a can of ginger ale out of the fridge. She slapped the compromise down on the island in front of Troy. "OK? Now get up to your room and get that homework going."

Troy popped the top of his ginger ale, took a long gulp, and exhaled a humongous, rolling belch.

"Gross!" Mel and I groaned in unison. Satisfied, Troy grinned, grabbed the bag of cheese doodles, and clomped off down the hallway.

Mel listened for the fade of Troy's footsteps on the stairs and the slam of his bedroom door. Then she turned to me, all serious. "Phone book," she said, like a surgeon requesting a scalpel. I handed her the book.

Mel flipped the yellow pages open to A, skimmed the page with her finger, stopped at "Abortion Services," and wrote down a couple of numbers.

Troy rushed into the kitchen, startling us both.

"What now?" Mel snarled.

"Jeez, I forgot my stupid backpack. Sor-reee!"

Troy hoisted his pack over his shoulder and lugged it out of the kitchen. "Girls!" he mumbled, walking away.

"Too cute," I said. On a day when my world looked pretty bleak, Troy made me smile.

Mel snorted. "Yeah he is. A real laugh riot." She finished her cracker and took a swallow of cranberry juice before picking up the phone.

"Well, here we go." Mel closed her eyes and made a sign of the cross, then punched in the first number.

"Is this the Crisis Pregnancy Clinic? ... Uh, yes ... What's that?... No thanks, I don't need a free pregnancy test. ... Yes, I'm sure. I mean, yeah, it was definitely positive. I'm wondering if you have RU-486 there. ... Oh. ... Uh-huh ..." Mel frowned and her face flushed. "No, I hadn't heard that, and I don't believe it either. Who does your research anyway? ... Yeah? Well, I know exactly what I want to do. Terminate. ... Yes ... What? What exactly are you implying? ... Yes, as a matter of fact I have given it 'a great deal of thought,' thank you very much." Mel sat up straighter on the stool. "Yeah, I'm sure you do, and hey, you know what? In case you haven't noticed, you're listed under the *wrong* category in the phone book!"

Mel clicked the phone off and smacked her own forehead. "Ugh. My bad. I should have had a clue with that name! It was an anti-choice clinic masquerading as a pro-choice one. Oh yeah they have free pregnancy tests, and free maternity clothes to lend you too! Jeez, I barely asked her anything, and she started in on all the reasons why I should *have* the baby. How it was morally wrong for me to think in any other direction. BSers! Putting themselves under 'Abortion Services.' They use all these sneaky phrases to make women feel guilty. And the bitch of it is, it works! Like 'abortion on demand.' Right! I'm sure women go in and smash their fists down on the front desk and yell, 'I *demand* an abortion!' It totally sucks. They fool girls into calling and then guilt-trip the hell out of them." I watched Mel ignite, her energy was on fire.

I got really quiet.

Mel touched my arm. "Hey you, we're not letting them get to us. OK?"

I shook my head no, completely unsure. It really seemed like they'd gotten to Mel.

Mel looked back at the open phone book, winked at me and dialed another number. "Planned Parenthood, definitely a safer bet ... Um, hi. I was just wondering, you do abortions there, right? ... OK. Can I ask some questions? ... Do you have RU-486? ... What's that? ... Mifeprex? ... OK, but that's like the same thing, right? ... Um, about four weeks, wait," Mel looked at me with question-mark eyes. I held up five fingers.

"Closer to five, I think." Mel said. "Uh-huh. That's great." Mel gave a thumbs-up. "OK, yeah. What's the price, please? ... Oh. Uh-huh, and does that include both visits? ... What? ... Oh. ...

Uh-huh, OK. … Yeah." Mel made a face and gave a thumbs-down. "OK. Well, thanks a lot. … No, that's all for now. Bye."

Mel clicked the phone off and put it down. She picked another cracker up from her plate, turned it to the edge with thicker cheese, and chomped down, chewing and thinking.

"She sounded nice, but the mondo bummer is that we're in a parental-consent state. ID required. Hey, maybe we can fix you up with a fake one?" Mel's mind seemed to be clicking away on that idea.

"No way I can pass for eighteen."

Mel scanned me, took a long sip of her cranberry juice and chewed on the ice.

I was right. No doubt.

"We'll think of something," she said. "I can't believe how much info she gave me over the phone. She never even asked my age."

"So, it's not a regular abortion?"

"No. It's a medical one. They give you some pills, you wait, then you get your period. Done." Mel grinned, like she'd solved all my problems with a phone call. I wished she had.

"What if it is living or has feelings?"

"Jeez, don't do a Jenna on me. Or an Evil Elaine, God forbid." Mel bowed her head, scowled at me, and crossed herself in a perfect Sister Elaine imitation. I wanted to laugh, but I couldn't.

"They've been using this stuff in Europe for, like, fifteen years or something. Women there just get a prescription from their doctors and get it filled, anywhere. No prob."

"How do you know all this?"

"The Internet. I've heard my mother talking with some of her friends about it, too."

"It sounds kind of scary."

"Doesn't having a baby sound scarier? Jeez, don't let the Church or anyone else talk you into ruining your entire life for one mistake. You're only fifteen. Come on, Kara, choose yourself. You're smarter than this. You are."

I didn't feel particularly smart.

"What's the cost?"

"About four hundred bucks."

I winced.

"Can't we count on a little contribution from Jake Dodson?"

"Oh sure, maybe his new girlfriend, Sedona, will split it with him. Ugh, I really hate that name."

"Agreed, fairly pretentious. Don't you think Jakey boy's the teensiest bit responsible here? Shouldn't he at least be coming up with half?"

"For one thing, I never want to see or talk to him again. Not in this lifetime or the next, if we get one. No way I want him to know anything about this either. OK?"

"O-*kay.*" Mel ripped a piece of paper from the phone message pad and started calculating.

"I can maybe scrape together a hundred. You?"

"About the same. Plus, my father keeps emergency cash stashed in his night table drawer. I could get a hundred or so from there. I don't think he'd miss it. Not right away."

"Risky," Mel said, but she added that to her tally.

"I don't care. I'd rather be caught stealing and say I'd blown it on shopping than ask his permission to have an abortion."

Mel interrupted her calculations. "True, most definitely. But we're still short about a hundred. Shit, I forgot to ask if there was tax."

"What about the parental-consent thing? No way I can ask them, Mel. Impossible." My stomach was gurgling. I opened the refrigerator, searching the shelves for something to quiet the sounds.

"Hey, what about my mom? She could give consent for you!"

It was a flash of genius. Mel got up and boogied around the island, throwing kisses to a fantasy audience of admirers.

"Wow. Do you think she would?" I found a ginger ale and popped it open.

"Sure. Mom is totally pro-choice. She'll understand. Besides, she's like a second mother to you anyway. Right?"

I nodded and blew across the top of my soda can to make a whistling sound. Maybe Sherry would help. She certainly wouldn't freak out like my parents. My stomach felt calmer; I was hopeful.

"I'll ask her, like, as soon as she gets home from work, OK?" Mel was so excited.

"But what if she tells my parents?" I said.

Mel thought about that, then shook her head.. "No, no way. She'd never."

Still, Sherry was a grown-up, and a mother. Cool, yeah, but maybe not that cool. "Let me think about it, OK? Don't say anything yet."

"You're the boss," Mel smiled.

I downed the rest of my soda, rinsed the can, and tossed it into the recycling bin by the pantry.

Mel walked me to the back door.

I hugged her. "Thanks, Mel, you're the best."

"Don't worry, OK? Everything's gonna work out. Call me later."

There were four blocks between my house and Mel's. I took my time, in no hurry to reach my destination.

The day was warm for March. Patches of mushy, leftover snow from the last storm peeked out here and there from the shady places of the dry, yellow-brown lawns.

A woman with a little girl and an infant in a stroller passed me on the sidewalk. The little girl waved to me and called out a hello. Her mother smiled. The baby was asleep, wrapped in a blanket and wearing a white hat with a blue tassel on his tiny head. I looked away from them. The hideous lie I was living was bigger every day. As the cells and tissue in me grew, the knowledge that I was a sneak and a liar did, too.

My grandmother used to say "This too shall pass." She would say it about my hurt feelings if some kid was mean to me on the playground or the time when I had the double-bad case of chicken pox.

Grandma was right. With time, things usually had a way of working out.

But my past felt like it was right on top of my present, crushing me. Like it would never pass or let me out from under it.

Grandma, where are you? I wished she could hug me. I wanted to hear her say that all this would pass and be OK.

Step on a crack, break your mother's back. I scoped out every crack in the cement and stepped carefully across each one. I couldn't stand for Mom to hate me, to be disappointed in me. That felt like death.

What if taking RU-486 was a mortal sin? What if I really was killing something that was part me and part Jake? These ideas ticked through my brain incessantly, no matter how hard I tried not to think about them.

"Hey, Kara! Hi!"

Ugh. A waving Emma Moriarity and her bratty dog were trotting up the sidewalk, directly in my path.

It was too late for me to cross the street or pretend I didn't see them.

"Hey, your mother and mine are working together."

"They are?"

"Yeah, my Mom says they're going to plan this big fund-raiser for Bruce Statler. He's pro-life, you know. I was helping Xerox some invitations yesterday. You should have come. It was so fun!"

"I'll bet."

I imagined Emma's mother in her chunky bracelets and one of her gaudy turquoise necklaces stuffing envelopes, full of smug self-satisfaction. Emma was going to turn out just like her.

"We had pizza, too. Oh, and guess what? I'm going out for JV cross-country."

"Yeah, I heard."

"You did? How?" Emma seemed elated to have made it to the edge of my radar screen. Sparky sniffed and proceeded to lift his leg on one of the massive oak trees in Mrs. Connelly's front yard.

"Your mother told me."

"She did? When?"

"I don't know. A while ago."

I let out a small sigh. Talking to a twelve-year-old about her extracurricular choices wouldn't be high on my list under normal circumstances. I thought of Mel's nickname for her: Emma "Morality." It made me smile.

"I'd better go. I've got a ton of homework," I said, moving away.

"OK, bye Kara."

Emma trotted away with her beloved Sparky beside her. Tomorrow, she'd tell all her seventh-grade friends we were tight. Ugh.

Crossing my front lawn, I wondered about Emma, whether she had gotten her first period, if she knew anything at all about anything. Highly doubtful. Lucky Emma.

My mother opened the front door before I even made it up to the front steps.

"Hey, Mom."

"Hi. Stop at Mel's?"

"Yeah."

"You just missed your dad. He told me to say good-bye." Mom gave me a peck on the cheek and touched my hair. "He had to go down to Colorado Springs again, remember?"

"Oh, yeah. Sorry, I forgot."

I was forgetting a lot of things lately and remembering too much of what I wanted to forget.

"My day was packed with phone lists and campaign calls. How about yours?"

She was a happy and perky mother, wanting to hear happy things about my day.

"Fine. The usual." I put my backpack down on the landing, hating my lies and the ugly ease with which they fell from my mouth. No, this day wasn't fine. It was hideous like every day since I'd snuck out with Jake. Since I ate those Jell-O shots and walked up those stairs. I wanted to tell her.

"Want a snack?" Mom asked, heading toward the kitchen. "Boy, listen to my voice. I've been on the phone way too much. I still have more envelopes to stuff. Feel like helping?"

It would crush her to know the truth. Crush her.

"No thanks, I had something at Mel's. Sorry I can't help with the mailing. I've got way too much homework. Need to get on it."

No way I could stomach looking at those flyers, those pictures and slogans. I headed up to my room. I hadn't even told Mel. Not the whole truth about everything. What a fool I'd been. How used and stupid I felt every day, every night. All the time.

"I'll call you when dinner's ready," Mom said.

I realized what a good thing it was that Mel had never asked me for any details. I'd have lied to her, too.

After two hours of supreme effort, not a word of *Hamlet* had penetrated my stressed out brain. My feeble attempts at creating a study sheet had ended in complete failure. Too little sleep and too much worry were taking a wicked toll on my GPA.

The phone rang. Caller ID showed Mel's number, so I grabbed it.

"Hey."

"Hey. You sitting down?" Mel asked.

I sat down on the edge of my bed and then fell back against my quilt, stretching my arms out on either side of me. Like Jesus, crucified.

"Lying down, actually," I replied, crooking the phone under my chin, glad to hear Mel's voice.

"Bad news." Mel said. She sounded scared.

I pulled myself back up to sitting with the bedpost. The crystal beads of the rosary bit into my palm.

"Ow. What?"

"Troy told Mom."

"Told her what?"

"What we talked about in the kitchen."

"No way. Shit!"

"All of it, the phone calls, the money. Everything."

"How?"

I took the rosary from the bedpost and squeezed the red enamel cross between my thumb and index finger.

"He must have eavesdropped, sat on the stairs stuffing his big mouth with cheese doodles. Guess he heard enough to figure it out. The little shit."

"Oh no. What did your mom say?"

"She was really mad. I thought she'd be way cooler. She said we should have come to her, like, right away. And besides, she says it would be illegal for her to give permission for you because she's not your real parent. They've got some law against that now. She said if you don't tell your parents, she has to."

I put the rosary down on my night table. A deep imprint of the cross remained on my thumb.

There were tears in Mel's voice. "I'm sorry. This sucks. I'm gonna kill Troy, I swear."

My chin hurt. I realized how hard I was pressing the phone against it and stopped.

"You still there?"

My heart was thumping hard. "Yeah."

My mother called up to me, "Kara? Dinner in five."

"Tell them, Kara. You've got to. Better you than my mother. Besides, they're your parents. They have to love you no matter what. Right?"

Mel had no clue about my mother's involvement with the DLA, or Bruce Statler. No clue that my mother would hate me for this, not love me.

"Kara ...?"

"Yeah. OK, gotta go." I was numb. "See you, Mel." I clicked the phone off and put it down. Mel had just given me the worst news ever—with the exception of my positive pregnancy tests.

At least my father was away.

I had to tell my mother.

Tonight.

Telling Mom

It took me a long time to get from my room to the kitchen. I wished it could take me the rest of my life. The fourth step creaked when my foot touched down on it; so did the seventh. She had to love me no matter what. She had to love me no matter what. She would. She would.

My mother moved around the kitchen, from the island to the stove and back again, humming to herself—afloat in her safe and tidy world. I stood in the doorway, watching her.

She had to love me.

"Almost ready. I'll put the pasta on in a minute. Can you set the table?"

I took a breath. She had to. Love me. Had to.

"Can we eat in the nook tonight?" I asked.

"Sure, if you'd like. Put the cheese out too. It's already grated on a plate in the fridge."

A stack of freshly sealed Statler campaign envelopes sat in a neat pile next to the refrigerator. Mom was at the stove with her back to me. I pulled the plate of parmesan out of the fridge. It smelled like puke. My stomach tightened, and I felt faint.

I put the plate down next to the envelopes and held the edge of the counter to get my balance. "Can I have some mint tea? My stomach isn't so great."

"Before dinner or with?"

"Before. Please."

"Sure." Mom put the kettle on to boil and turned off the pot of water she was heating for the pasta.

I set two places in the nook.

Possible ways to begin the conversation thundered through my brain. Direct and just spit it out, get it over with fast? Or ease into it, kind of prepare her for what's coming? Maybe just talk about sneaking out first? Maybe say it while we were eating?

No. Don't tell her during dinner. Both of us might barf.

I dropped down in the nook. My body shivered. I suddenly felt cold.

"Mom, there's something I have to tell you."

The crack in my voice pulled my mother right to the table.

I needed to say things just right, to soften the blow, but I couldn't say one word. All I could do was look at her.

"Sweetie, what's the matter?" Mom reached across the table and touched my hand. "What is it?"

"I'm in trouble."

"Oh, no. Did you get a detention? Are we going to get another interim report?" My mother sat opposite me, her face moist from hovering above the steamy pots. She brushed her bangs from her forehead. "Tell me. It's OK." Mom folded her hands on the table, ready to listen, her round, wide-set eyes a mirror of my own.

I loved her, and I was about to break her heart.

"No, with a boy. That kind."

The shrill whistle of the kettle filled the silent kitchen. Mom stood up, on autopilot. She set a mug and a mint tea bag down in front of me. She turned the burner off, brought the kettle over, and filled my mug with hot water, then took another mug, put a tea bag in it for herself, poured again, and took her seat. I blew across the top of my tea and reached for the pot of honey in the center of the table. Everything was happening in slow motion.

"You've met a boy?"

Had she heard me? *Trouble ... With A Boy!* Mom seemed too normal and calm. Was I in a dream, or what?

The hint of a smile crossed mom's lips. "I'm glad. Are you saying you want to go out with him and you'd like me to talk to your dad?"

Clueless. Maybe she didn't want to hear. Maybe this was all too far from her version of normal to process.

"No, way past that. Too late for that."

I wiped my eyes with the back of my wrist, took a deep breath, and let it blow out of me. With a silent shrug, my eyes pleaded with Mom to take over, to somehow intuit what I had to say, to not make me be the one to say the word *pregnant.*

I pointed at my stomach. "I'm late."

Mom put her hand over her mouth, her deep brown eyes full of shock and disbelief.

"Oh God. You're not ... pregnant? Kara? That's impossible!"

I nodded my head, a firm yes, and spooned honey into my tea. I stirred and stirred, the spoon rattled against my mug.

Mom breathed in sharply, like she'd been punched. Her mind must have been racing behind her arched brows; she was probably thinking she'd misunderstood me or heard me wrong, that this was a really bad joke. My terrified eyes told her otherwise.

"Oh. Sweetie. No."

It was surreal sitting in our breakfast nook, waiting for my tea to cool, and having a conversation about pregnancy with my mother. My pregnancy.

"Who is he? Who's the boy?" she asked.

"I don't want to talk about him, OK? This is about me and what I need to do." I sounded like Mel, but only for a second.

Mom put her face in her hands and slumped over. "Oh, Kara. How did this happen? How?"

I wanted to kick myself for hurting her.

My mother sat up and slid her hand across the table, reaching for me.

"The usual way," I murmured.

Niagara Falls struck; I couldn't stop the shoulder-shaking sobs. I pulled a tissue from the box on the counter and blew my nose.

My mother seemed overwhelmed, unable to take it all in.

"How can this be, Kara? You're not even dating. You have an early curfew; you've hardly ever been out at night." My mother wrapped her arms across her stomach, rocking herself back and forth and holding her eyes steady on mine.

I wanted—and really needed—someone to step up and comfort me, to tell me that somehow everything would be all right, that this could be handled and we'd solve all my problems. But Mom, my own mom, couldn't; she was trying, but she was in shock.

"I don't understand," was all she could say.

"I snuck out, Mom, and I lied about things. I did, and I'm so sorry. I really am. It was stupid and really dumb. I hate myself."

My mother got up and came around to my side of the nook. She squeezed in next to me and put her arm around my trembling shoulders. I released a giant sigh and leaned into her.

"I really do, I hate myself."

"Don't, Kara, don't say that. Please."

"Dad is going to kill me!" The whine in my voice, the hysterical wail of it, sounded gross. I knew I was acting like a little kid, but I couldn't stop myself.

"No, don't say that, don't even think it. You're so wrong about him. Who's the boy? How did you meet him?"

"He's nobody. A total jerk!"

"Have you told him?"

I met her eyes. "Yeah, and he said for me to get an abortion."

"Oh, sweetie." Mom was quiet for a long minute digesting that. She stared at her steaming mug of tea. Her baby, had sex with a boy. And was pregnant. I had disappointed her beyond anything either of us could ever have imagined.

My eyes drifted to the stuffed Statler envelopes right next to us, on the counter. Ready to mail. *Choose Life, Choose Life.*

"Is it that boy who called a few weeks ago? When you were home sick? That one who wouldn't leave his name?"

"Yes. 'Called.' As in past tense. We are so over, Mom. Done. Please, I don't want to talk about him. Don't try to make me."

Mom put her hand under my chin and turned my face to hers, her watery eyes penetrated mine. "Not completely, Kara. You're pregnant. That's real. That's not over."

"But I want it to be. It has to be. You have to help me, please! I can't eat; I can't sleep or study. Anything. I just want to die." I meant every word, and it scared me.

My mother leaned back against the seat and wiped the heel of her hand quickly under each eye. She hardly ever cried. I hadn't seen her cry since Grandma's funeral.

"I don't care if Sister Elaine thinks it's a sin, if you and Dad do, or Jean Moriarity, the nuns at school—anybody! I don't even care if I go to Hell because I'm already *in* Hell. I'm already being punished, every second of every day."

Mom exhaled and put her hand on her forehead. "Shouldn't we at least talk to his parents?"

"No! I've never even met them. Mom, I hate this guy, I really do. You can't make me have his baby. I'll run away. I'll take poison. I swear I will!"

Mom looked into my eyes, anxious. "Please don't say things like that, Kara. Please. Do you love him?"

"No! He's a creep, and he already has another girl. Some stupid blond cheerleader from Cherry Creek." My mouth quivered over the words. I sounded so frantic, so desperate.

So dumped.

My mother hugged me, pulling me close to her. "It's OK, honey, calm down. I'm here," she said. "It's always some blonde, isn't it? Just like in the movies."

Even though we were both crying, Mom and I laughed a little.

"When is Dad coming back?"

"In a few days."

"Please, don't tell him. Please. He'll freak out, he'll be so mad at me."

Mom sighed. "He loves you, much more than you know."

"Can we call Sherry? She knows what to do, where to go. Can we just call her? Please?"

"You told Sherry?"

I nodded. Another betrayal. How much more could she take? "Not really. Troy told her. He heard Mel and me talking about it. We were making some calls to a clinic." I blew my nose into my already soaked tissue. I was the worst daughter ever.

"A clinic?" Mom reached for the tissue box on the counter. She put it on the table and took one for herself.

"I'm sorry, Mom. Yeah, we called Planned Parenthood. I was afraid to tell. I thought you'd be so mad. I thought you'd hate me. You're so into all the DLA stuff, working for Statler and all that."

Mom was staring at the design on the side of the tissue box, silent. Reality was setting in.

"I'm sorry, so sorry, Mom. I hate how I've let you down."

"Oh, honey, come on. I love you always, no matter what. And so does your father. We'll figure this out. We will."

We sat in the nook for a long time, my mother holding me. Neither of us felt like getting up from the nook or eating pasta.

Telling Mom was like lifting a boulder off my heart. No matter what happened now, at least I could breathe.

My Worst Nightmare
(Wasn't so Bad)

I tossed and turned, tossed and turned. It was the most broken sleep I'd ever had. Dreams, nightmares, sweaty sheets. Dreams of Jake, of death, of murderous guilt.

Why me? What did I do to deserve this? I hated me and I woke up with that thought, opened my eyes to "I hate me." I stared at the ceiling with those words burning into my brain.

And he was there.

"Kara?"

My father. The person I was most afraid to tell, the curfew monster, was in my room. Mom must have called him last night. Late. She'd betrayed me.

I closed my eyes and rolled over. Asleep. That was it, I was still asleep. This was a bad dream, a nightmare.

"Honey? You awake?" The voice sounded strange, unlike my father's. It was softer and easier than I'd heard it in a long time.

"The three of us need to talk—you, me, and your mom." No, my father always called her "your mother."

This had to be a dream. I rolled over and squinted a peek. Yes, right there. My father was standing by my bed. Then he was squatting, eye level and close.

"What time?" I mumbled, slitting my eyes open enough to see my clock.

Nine o'clock! I threw my covers off. "I'm late!"

"No, no school today. Your mom already called."

I sat up and took shallow breaths in and out, in and out, staring at him. Blinking, and realizing—he knows. He *knows*.

But my father didn't look mad. His eyes were soft, watery, and incredibly sad. He stood up and walked to the door of my room. He turned at the doorway. "Get dressed and come down to the den, all right?"

His tone was serious, but kind.

"Kara, you're going to be OK. Believe that." He closed the door gently behind him. No slam.

With my eyes on the door, and my feet dangling off the edge of my bed, I felt for the left slipper and then the right. Mind-crunching anxiety was closing in on me.

They knew. And now they wanted to talk.

My parents were both sitting on the beige sofa in the den; a tufted throw pillow was behind Mom's back. Dad sat so straight, right on the edge of the sofa, his eyes were mottled with worry. Or was it guilt? Why should he feel guilty? Everything was my fault. Mine.

"Sit down, honey," my father said. It was a soft, caring, quiet voice, not his courtroom bluster voice or the firm, angry tone he used at home with me.

The *Denver Post* was lying on the coffee table with the sports page face up. DODSON PULLS IT OUT! was sprawled across the top of the page over a giant picture of Jake swishing the ball through the net.

Jake was right there, in full color, in front of my parents. He was staring up at them, mocking them.

The phone was face down on the coffee table next to a pad of paper and a pen. I slumped into the overstuffed chair opposite them. A dark cloud of silence filled the room. I wasn't ready for this talk. My hate-filled eyes bored into my mother.

"Honey, I called your dad because it was the right thing to do. He's your father. He deserves to know."

"You lied to me."

"Kara, I didn't. I know you asked, but I never told you I wouldn't call him. We both love you and want to help you."

"Why didn't you want me to know? Why?" The lines around Dad's eyes had softened, and his tone was gentle, but no doubt he was hurt, really hurt.

Mom put her hand on my father's arm. "Your dad is upset, of course, but he's also, well … he'll tell you."

"We need to decide what to do and how to help you. All of us, together, as a family," he said.

"Help me? You're always mad at me. You never let me do anything or go anywhere. I thought you'd ground me for life. Of course I didn't want you to know."

I chewed on one of my nails and then stopped. I held my hand in my lap, staring at it. "I'm sorry. I didn't really know what to do. I was scared." I looked up at them. "I guess that's fairly obvious."

"So are we, Kara. So are we."

"But Dad, you're never scared."

"Well, I …" My father took a deep breath and dropped his head. He held his knotted hands together between open knees. "Your Aunt Sarah …," he began. His face lifted, and his eyes linked with mine. We sat in a quiet pause with him just looking at me. Uncomfortable. My father never struggled for words. Never. I waited.

"When I was ten, Sarah got into trouble with a boy. Pregnant. She was sixteen and a junior in high school."

I sat forward in my seat. I had no idea. None.

"Well, our family was Catholic, very Catholic. My father never considered trying to get help for her from a willing doctor, which is what had to be done in those days. No, instead of that, my father blamed her." Dad's tone was acidic, bitter.

"So, Sarah defied my father and dropped out of high school to marry the boy. It was a small ceremony; she was about five months along and showing … Maybe she believed she was in love. I don't know." My father clenched his hands and then opened them on his kneecaps. "As I think of all this now, she may have done it partly to get back at my father because he'd been so … strict."

"Aunt Sarah never talked about her husband. I always wondered about him, but it never seemed like it was OK to ask her," I said.

"Well, he was an abusive guy with a serious drinking problem. Sarah was a single mother with three kids under the age of six by the time she was twenty-two. No job, no education. Her husband was a high school dropout, a few years older than she was. He worked construction jobs on and off. I think the idea of Sarah having an education was a threat. I half think he kept making her pregnant so she couldn't go back to school. Needless to say, it didn't work out well for her."

"What happened?"

"Sarah finally threw him out. My father wouldn't hear of her divorcing, of course; he wanted her to stay in the marriage. At least Sarah got the bum out of the house. I was eighteen by then and so damn proud of her for standing up for herself and her kids. After I finished law school, I helped her out with money for therapy, whatever she and her kids needed."

"Maybe that's why Aunt Sarah got sick. The stress," I said.

My father's body sagged against the back of the sofa, formless, fightless, giving in to a sadness he had never let me see.

"I can't say for sure whether it caused her cancer, but I do believe that it broke her heart and spirit."

"Why didn't you ever tell me?"

"Your cousins were pretty much grown by the time you came along. When you were little, we didn't think you needed to know, and you were only ten when Sarah died."

I sat motionless, absorbing every syllable.

My father's raw, unfamiliar facial expressions were difficult to watch, too vulnerable and open. Too real. Dad shook his head back and forth. "I'm telling you now because I hope that you may be able to understand where I was coming from, why I've been so strict and protective." He let out an enormous sigh. "It's because of Sarah that I wanted you to go to an all-girls school through high school. Because of her that I didn't want you dating too young or going out at night."

"Jeez, but home felt like a prison. I had to escape. I couldn't breathe."

My father had tears in his eyes. Tears. "I'm so sorry, honey."

I got up, went to him, and hugged him. "It's OK, Dad."

"Kara, there's nothing OK about this. We've got a mess on our hands. Your mom tells me you won't even tell us who the boy is or how you met him."

I stood up from the hug. My father ran the back of his hand across his forehead and sat up on the edge of the sofa. "And, I feel like this is all my fault." His voice collapsed on the last word.

"No, Dad, I was wrong. I broke the rules. I shouldn't have."

Mom pulled me down between them on the sofa and put her arm around me.

"I've made mistakes, pushed too hard." Dad was choked up but trying hard to hold it in. "God, I only wanted to keep you safe. That's all I was ever thinking about." He put his fist to his mouth.

No one said anything for a long moment.

The grandfather clock in the living room was ticking, ticking. Dad wiped under each of his eyes with his thumb.

"Dad, are *we* very Catholic?" My voice was barely there.

My father looked at my mother, but she stared at her lap. There was a tense void between them.

Dad looked at me. "Honey, I don't know the answer to that, but I guess we're going to find out."

Parental Combustion

“**S**o, we're right back to it's murder, plain and simple. Is that what you're saying?”

“That's not what I meant, and you know it.”

Hot words bored through my muddled tangle of dreams. Booming angry voices slid up the stairs and into my ears from the living room below. I sat up in my bed, listening to the raised voices, the combusting tempers.

My mother and father?

“You've made her so damn frightened with all this DLA business that she won't even give us the boy's name. How did we get this far off track, Maggie? Tell me, how?”

I got up from my bed and ballet-walked on the balls of my feet through my room and down the carpeted hallway. I perched myself on the top stair to listen.

“Please keep your voice down, Bill. You'll wake her.”

My father's forceful exhale blew across the living room. “All right. All right.”

I imagined his face, his arched brows, his index finger smoothing the creases on his forehead.

"Come on, Bill, sit down. Please."

I pictured Mom sitting on the sofa and patting the cushion next to her, coaxing him with her eyes.

"It's just that working on the Statler campaign has made all this especially hard for me." Mom's voice went very soft.

"And that's exactly why I didn't want you to do it," Dad said.

He was really mad. I edged myself down two steps and tucked my head below the edge of the banister, peering through the white wood slats and across the entryway into the living room.

"Why? Were you *expecting* this to happen to her? You never told me not to get involved again. Not once." Mom's eyes stayed on the sofa as she ran a finger along the brown piping on the beige cushion. "Please, Bill, let's not blame each other."

"Well, I certainly implied it. Many times. You know how I feel about the DLA—and the whole condemning, judgmental ideology of the pro-life movement. It's too black-and-white for me. I felt that way when you got involved before, and I made no secret of it. You knew all about the holy chaos that Sarah's life became and my feelings about that. Not a thing has changed."

"Yes, it has. Kara's in trouble." Mom's head came up when she said that, and I thought she might see me. Holding my breath, I inched back up to the top step and out of sight.

"Yes. More than 'in trouble,'" my father said. "She's pregnant. Doesn't that make all the difference? For us? Shouldn't it? She's our daughter, the only one we'll ever have. The least you can do is hear these people out tomorrow."

There was not a sound from Mom.

"Well, I'm going to go whether you come or not, and I'm going to ask Kara to come with me."

"I don't know. I don't know. Oh, I don't … Bill, please try to understand. I'm not trying to be difficult. I'm not. I'm just very confused. You know why I feel the way I do …"

"But I don't understand your confusion, OK? Where do you draw the line, Maggie? If not here and now for the sake of our only child, a fifteen-year-old sophomore in high school, then where the hell do you draw the line?"

Intense. A full-on, ugly, no-win had somehow wedged its way between my parents, thanks to me. They never really argued. Not like this. Not hard and mean. What if they got a divorce because of me, because of this idiotic, selfish thing I'd done? Giant tears glided down both sides of my face. I pressed two fingers against my quivering lips. I'd never forgive myself. Never.

Their voices became more hushed, muffled and confidential. I strained to hear what they were saying but couldn't pull in another word.

What if they were deciding to make me go away, to make me have a baby? What if I had to leave school for a year and give the baby up for adoption to some Catholic foundling home and wonder about it forever and never know?

I would hate them for that—hate them forever.

With ragged nerves and a pounding headache I tiptoed back to bed. I'd totally wrecked my life, and now I was ruining theirs.

I squeezed my eyes shut and pulled the comforter up over my head. But the darkness couldn't stop my brain from spiraling through the fear. Worries and fears about the future, about the total chaos that was my life. What was going to happen to me now?

The question spun out of my mind into the darkness, unanswered.

Whose Choice Is It, Anyway?

My father wanted a meeting. Of the minds, religion, the law? All three?

No. A meeting with some people from Catholics for Choice. Dad had called Sherry, and she'd set us up with some friends of hers in a flash.

My mother, father, and I were sitting in the living room of total strangers, Larry and Mary. My parents sat together on their sofa; I was in a red wingback chair a few feet away from them. Nerves had increased my appetite to the tenth power. I'd already scarfed down half of my second giant chocolate croissant.

The four adults kept talking and talking. Half an hour of embarrassingly intimate topics had already sped by—the growing rate of teens who are sexually active, rising teen pregnancy rates, birth control, and abstinence only education in schools. Sex ed, information about birth control? That didn't exist at Saint Ursula's.

The bulk of their conversation only made it to the edge of my ears; it was swirling around my head, but not getting in. Then came the real focus—last but definitely foremost in all of our minds: the Church and abortion.

My ears perked.

"Some Catholics believe abortion can be morally justified only within specific circumstances," Larry said, "such as when a woman's life is at risk or when her health is endangered and in the case of incest or rape."

Larry's eyes moved back and forth between my mother and my father. Larry had a smooth, shiny head and a forest of salt-and-pepper eyebrows. His wire-rims had formed deep grooves on either side of his long, thin nose.

Please let them listen, I begged. Please. Please.

"Roughly 74 percent of Catholics believe it's possible to decide for oneself about issues such as birth control and abortion and to accept, at the least, a laissez-faire approach." Larry picked up his coffee and took a sip.

"That's a large percentage, and these are people who consider themselves good Catholics," Mary added.

Heavy-set and blue-eyed, Mary smiled often and refilled everyone's coffee cups. Her graying hair was pinned up on the back of her head with an ornate silver clip edged with tiny copper roses. It reminded me a little of Grandma's mirror.

"Where does papal law stand?" Dad asked.

Ugh. I concentrated on the croissant flakes and making them fall from my mouth into the napkin on my lap. I didn't want to think about papal law or the Church or the nuns at Saint Ursula's.

"There has been no dogma passed down through the centuries specifically stating that abortion is a sin," Larry replied.

"What about excommunication?" My mother's wide-open eyes were anxious. "I'm sorry, Larry, but a lot of what you're saying is in complete opposition to what I know and what I've been taught."

I hated all those words: dogma, papal law, sin, excommunication.

"Taught. That's the key, Maggie. We were not only trained in our beliefs but told how to *think*. We all grew up believing a lot of things as Catholics; we accepted the teachings of priests and nuns and bishops without question. On faith. These days, they're even telling us who we should and shouldn't vote for."

Dad glanced at her, but Mom's eyes were fixed on Larry; she was pressing her teeth against her bottom lip, concentrating.

"Well, over the last decade or so, Mary and I began to ask ourselves why we accepted so much and asked so few questions. We began to re-think what we'd learned in our fifty-odd years of being Catholic, especially after these last few years, rife with sordid disclosure of the abuse scandals and what not ... you know?" Larry shook his head. "Frankly, Mary and I are not prepared to let the Roman hierarchy sit in judgment of us; we're not about to let them tell us what we must believe about a woman's private reproductive life or how to vote." Larry looked at Mary and smiled. "It's been quite a journey, hasn't it, hon?"

Mary reached for Larry's hand and squeezed his in her own. She smiled at my mother and added, "I can tell you I didn't fully agree with all of this at first."

After looking at them for what felt like the zillionth time, I finally recognized Larry and Mary. I'd seen them at Mass lots of times. They were in our parish.

"So, you're saying that you have questioned Catholic dogma, faith, the basic tenets of the Baltimore Catechism that we all memorized in elementary school ... the pope himself?" Mom was incredulous. "You're just throwing it all out?"

"That is not what I heard him say, Maggie." My father was really tense.

I put the croissant down, my appetite was gone; I wanted to hear every word.

If I had to go through with this pregnancy to stay in the Church, to be a good Catholic, then I'd leave in a nanosecond. No one would have to kick me out.

"No, I certainly haven't thrown everything out, Maggie, but I have questioned my beliefs and my faith. I've done some research."

Larry leaned forward in his chair. "Here's the reality: Most Catholics believe in exceptions when it comes to banning abortion."

"Certainly when they are asked anonymously," Mary added.

"Yes, that's true." Larry continued, "When surveyed, only 13 percent were strictly by the book, following every word that their priest, their bishop, or the pope decrees. Let me ask you this, both of you. How many Catholics do you think still use the rhythm method?"

Larry waited for my parents to respond. Mom straightened her skirt and shrugged. Dad had a blank look, thinking.

"If I'm not mistaken, birth control is still absolutely forbidden by the Catholic Church, even to protect oneself from sexually transmitted diseases. Yet, does one commonly see families coming to Mass with seven-plus children in tow? Not like they did when I was a boy."

Dad looked at Mom. "Can't argue with him there, can we, Maggie?"

Mom didn't look at him or answer. A solid block of tension filled the space between my parents. My father scratched the side of his ear and cleared his throat.

Larry plowed ahead, unaware. Maybe he didn't notice how uptight they were because they'd been stressed for the entire meeting.

"So, once one accepts the idea that there can be exceptions for birth control, why stop there? What about abortion and the reproductive rights of women? The question really becomes who gets to decide where and when the exceptions will be made. Well, I'll tell you, if it's *my* life, then it's going to be me."

My mother, my father, and Larry sat stone still and looked at one another like three breathing statues.

"Would you like another pastry, Kara?" Mary asked.

"No, thank you. I'm stuffed."

Mary took a small square of sugar from a cut glass bowl and dropped it into her cup. The spoon clinked against the china as she stirred. "Women, including Catholic women, can and must be trusted to make good decisions about their reproductive lives, about how many children they choose to bear, and when. They don't need micromanaging from the pope or the states they live in."

"Or from the federal government, for that matter. God help us." Larry shook his head.

My father sipped his coffee. He sighed and met my gaze; his eyes crinkled into a half-smile.

"More coffee for anyone? Shall I make a fresh pot?" Mary asked.

"Thank you, no." Dad leaned back against the sofa and put the flat of his hand softly on my mother's taut back. She startled and then adjusted herself. Her knit brow softened a little.

Larry picked up a booklet from a small pile on the coffee table and handed it to my father. "Everything we've talked about is right here."

Dad put his cup down and took it. "Well, we don't want to take up any more of your day. Thank you, Larry, and Mary. I really appreciate your meeting with us on such short notice. You've been very generous with your time."

Mom and I rose from our seats.

Larry and Mary shook hands with my parents. They were starting and finishing each other's sentences.

"Sherry's a great friend …"

"—and we're more than glad to help …"

"Yes, any way we can … feel free to call."

"Please, do check out the Web site …"

"—you'll find it very informative …"

Mary took my hand in hers and put her other hand over it. "Good luck to you, Kara. Please take a look at the Web site when you get a chance. There's a section there for young people, too."

Mary pressed my hand, and I pressed back. "Thanks, I will."

But there was no way I could think about Web sites or dogma or the pope. I couldn't think about anything right then but getting my parents' permission to go to the clinic.

Silence filled the Mercedes for the ten-minute ride back to our house. Each one of us was lost in our own thoughts; no one offered a penny for anyone else's like Grandma used to do.

We walked across the backyard and single-filed into the kitchen. My dad put the Catholics for Choice pamphlet down on the island.

He poured himself a glass of water and sat down in the nook. Mom sat down across from him.

I poured myself some milk and leaned against the counter, watching and waiting. Hoping.

Dad breathed deeply, sighed, and said, "So. Here's how I see things …"

Mom opened her mouth, but my father put his finger up. "Just hear me out, Maggie, please."

She closed her mouth and sat back.

"Is the Church going to know what we, as a family, decide to do?" he asked her. "Do they have any right to know that we are making this decision?"

He gazed in my direction, asking for my opinion, too.

No one moved or said a word.

Dad pressed his index finger over the deep furrow between his eyebrows, smoothing it. "What do you want, Maggie? If you really want to have a consultation with Father Miller and get his input we can do that."

Mom was silent, thinking.

"No, I think we both know exactly what he's going to tell us to do. But I just feel awful about this, Bill. I can't help it. What will I say to the people at DLA or to Jean Moriarity? All the people I've been working with on the campaign. What are they going to think?" She let out a long, heavy exhalation.

"Who cares what they think? And how will they know unless you tell them? This is our family, our daughter. *We* decide what to do, Maggie. We do. They have no right to judge us or to coerce us in any direction about this. They have no right even to know that we are dealing with this crisis. None." His words seemed angry but his voice remained calm. My father put his hand around his water glass and moved it back and forth on the table.

"You know what?" He looked evenly at Mom. "I don't want to vote for Bruce Statler, and I'm not going to."

A challenge. A face-off.

"I just don't like the guy—who he is or what he stands for, and I can't even pretend to. Not anymore." My father's head went up and then down. Final. It was like my parents were all alone in the kitchen then, as if I didn't exist. My blood began to beat hard in my ears.

My mother broke the silence. She sat up with a quiet grin. I thought she'd lost it, reached some kind of limit. I really thought that she was going to crack.

"You know," Mom began, "quite honestly? I'm not really wild about Statler either."

My father registered shock. "What are you saying? You've worked like a dog for the man."

"I don't know. It just seems that the more I've seen him and listened to him and even spent time in personal conversation with him, the more I can't ... the more I find him to be ..." Mom hesitated and then blurted the words out. "Well, if I were to be completely honest about it, I think he's an arrogant, rigid ... fool."

What?! I was stunned. It was obvious my father was too.

My parents exchanged blank stares for a long moment.

"OK," Mom shrugged. "Call me stubborn and intractable. It's true. I don't switch gears easily and never have. And, well, I guess, in essence, I just haven't wanted to admit that I was working so hard for someone I basically don't like."

Silence, tension, shock, nothingness; we were all frozen in the moment.

Then, my parents both exploded in a roar of laughter—hard, together laughter, in-on-the-same-joke laughter. Convulsive. The pro-life campaign of Bruce Statler had thrown my mother and father into hysterics. It was contagious, I couldn't help joining in a little. The anger and tension vanished from the kitchen.

Dad wiped away tears of laughter and motioned for me to come and sit with them. I squeezed in beside him in the nook. He reached across the table and touched Mom's hand. "Come on, Mag, we're not about to let Kara give birth in her second year of high school, are we?"

Mom was unreadable. Self-doubting judgments about sin, Hell, and the DLA were probably coursing through her, thoughts she wouldn't speak. Couldn't.

My father rubbed her knuckles with his thumb. "At this point, I just don't care what the Church wants from us, Maggie. I really don't."

He looked deeply into my mother's eyes.

It was totally bizarre, like our own personal *Twilight Zone*. Less than forty-eight hours ago, I'd snuck to Mel's house to call a clinic, terrified that my parents would find out. Especially my father.

"Kara?" he said. "What do you think? What do you want to do?"

The spotlight was on me. I hesitated, wanting to say everything just right.

"Well, I've been going crazy these last few weeks, not knowing what to do or what would happen if you or Mom found out. I thought about running away, going some place where they'd help me without your ever knowing."

They looked horrified, and sad.

I bit on my knuckle and stared out the window at a bird bobbing on a tree branch in our backyard. Then, softly, I said, "I was afraid I might actually have to … you know, that you might send me away and make me have it, or something."

"Never, honey. We'd never do that to you," Mom said, blinking. I hoped she wasn't going to cry.

My voice got even lower, quieter. "I know I'm not ready at all to, like, be a mother. I want to finish school and have a life of my own first before I even think about having a baby."

"Of course you do," Dad said. "We both want you to be ready, too, when the time is right." He smiled at Mom. "It's an enormous responsibility, raising a child."

"Yes, absolutely," Mom agreed.

My father took a long sip of water. He studied the thumbnail on his right hand as if it was a critical deposition for one of his cases. The three of us sat for what seemed like an eternity. Just sat there.

Time stood still.

"Well," Dad began. "I don't know whether I should be called a good Catholic or a bad one, but of one thing I am certain." My father's eyes traveled back and forth between my mother and me. "The way my father handled my sister Sarah's pregnancy ruined her life and hurt her children as well. I don't want to let the same thing happen again, not in our family. I can't." He looked up at the ceiling, his face dead serious. "Not for any reason, rule, or dogma."

Mom's blinks became tears. She didn't bother to wipe them away. Small, wet drops fell to the table in front of her. She finally pulled a tissue from her pocket and wiped her nose and eyes.

Dad reached across the table and took her hand in his. "I hope you won't fight me, Maggie. I really want us to stand together now, to decide and agree on this as one. More than anything, I want that. We don't have to feel great about it or happy about it or anything but solid … our own little accord. I can't bear to have any rifts between us … over this or anything."

My mother's head was moving back and forth, back and forth, a great sadness in her eyes. We sat through another long silence. Dad hung on to her hand.

Small beads of sweat erupted beneath my bangs. What were they thinking?

About me? Aunt Sarah? Or papal law? My heart raced; it galloped.

Then, Mom began to nod her head. It was a small, firm nod. "OK. I know. To end this now is what's best for Kara. I understand that. Really. I know, and I believe it. I do." Her head kept moving up and down with her words as if convincing herself of each one she spoke.

My question was answered.

My father turned to me. "Is this what you want, Kara?"

"Yes." I could barely say the word.

"I mean, I don't think we should wait any longer to make this decision, do you?" he asked.

"No." My voice was a whisper.

"Then we'll call the clinic today and make an appointment," my father said. "Agreed?"

"Yes, right," Mom said. It was a firm yes. This was really happening.

Dad squeezed Mom's hand. "I'll make the call if you want, Mag, if you'll feel more comfortable."

"All right. OK, you call." My mother seemed relieved.

"Well, that's that then," Dad said. "We have our decision."

Mom squeezed my father's hand, and then she reached over and took mine like the three of us were saying grace over it.

But nobody said "Amen."

The Clinic

The day was bright and sunny. But to me, the morning seemed as gray as my mother's Saab.

My father was leaving for work. He kissed Mom, then me, and climbed into his Mercedes. His window slid down. "Call me, OK?" he asked, and Mom nodded. Dad looked at me, a deep sadness behind his eyes. "We love you," he said. His lips twisted, he tried to turn them up at the ends in a smile for me, but his heartache was leaking through the car window as it glided up and closed.

I lifted my hand in a small wave. "I know."

My father held his hand up in a backward wave and drove his car away.

My thoughts curled in on themselves. I wanted this, I didn't, I wanted this, I didn't.

"We'd better get going," Mom said, opening her car door. I got in on the passenger side and sat motionless, frozen.

"Seatbelt," Mom said, fastening hers.

Seatbelt. Safety. Safe? My stomach clenched; I chewed on a hangnail until it bled. No, not safe.

"Nervous?" Mom asked.

"Yeah. Kind of."

"If it helps any, I am too." She pulled a packet of tissues from the side pocket of her door, handed me one, and turned the key in the ignition.

Mom's cell phone rang. She checked the Caller ID and hesitated, but then she picked up. "Hello? Hi Jean … No, I'm sorry, I can't, not today. … No, I'll be busy the whole day. … Right now is not a good time. Can I call you tomorrow? … Nothing, I'm fine. … Uh-huh. Thanks, bye."

I moistened the tissue with my tongue and held it tightly against my thumb until the bleeding stopped.

My mother turned off her cell and put it down on the console between us. "I'll deal with all that later. I will," she said, kind of to herself, and started the car. "I'm going to be right here, Kara, with you." She was backing her car out of the driveway. "All day."

"You and Dad have been so great, Mom. Thank you." I still couldn't believe how they'd pulled through for me. I felt lucky, and grateful.

The car turned out into the alley. My mother braked and faced me. "Sweetie, your dad and I love you. Always. Nothing can ever make that change or go away."

We walked together up to the two-story brick building with security bars on the windows. There were tall, bare oak trees on either side of the double-door entrance and a sign out front: Planned Parenthood.

Mom and I passed the sign without a word. I thought about the flyers I'd mailed and the words "death camp."

A dark-eyed young woman asked my mother for identification and pushed a sign-in sheet through a small slot in the bulletproof glass. Mom signed us in.

Getting into the clinic was like entering a bank vault or visiting a maximum-security prison. My heart pounded when we passed through the thick security door. This is legal, I told myself. I was here with my parents' permission.

But do I have my own? *Breathe*, I told myself.

I could do this. I had to.

Beyond the security door, an inner door swung wide.

"Hi, I'm Helen. Welcome," said a woman with a kind face, short gray hair, and red glasses. She touched my shoulder as I passed by her.

I felt shy and exposed. I'd had this huge secret, but once I was inside the clinic everyone who saw me knew exactly what the secret was without my saying a word.

Helen handed my mother a clipboard with paperwork to fill out and sign, parental permission forms and medical releases. Mom stopped to ask some questions. My mind floated off into the far corners of the room. I didn't want to listen to what they were saying, didn't want to hear the worry in my mother's voice.

The lights in the clinic were dim. I walked to the waiting area and sat down on a small sofa. A box of tissues and a pile of magazines sat on the end table next to me.

I reached for a magazine. My hand was trembling. Clasping both hands together, I squeezed them between my knees.

"Intense, huh?"

A girl with a diamond nose stud and short, choppy, hot pink hair sat down across from me. Her fingernails were painted black. She was grinning at me.

I only looked at her, obvious confusion showing on my face.

"You know, the whole thing. It's a big deal, deciding to come here and all that. Today is my final checkup. One big phew for me."

She was older than I was by a few years. Old enough to be here without a parent.

"Janine?" A woman in a sky blue lab coat came into the waiting area.

The girl smiled and stood up. "Don't worry," she said. "You'll be OK. They'll take care of you. It's all good here." She stepped away all bouncy, kind of happy even.

Maybe I'd be OK, too. Maybe.

We were called next. Mom and I spent a little while with a counselor in a small office near the waiting area. We were told about options and risks; we filled out and signed more forms. The counselor asked me, without Mom present, if I was sure "termination" was what I wanted. I told her yes, but I hated the sound of that word and all its synonyms.

Helen came to get us. "Kara and Maggie? Please come with me."

We followed her down a short hallway to an examining room.

I was asked to pull up my shirt to expose my stomach. Cold gel was smoothed over my belly as I lay on a paper-covered examination table. A long, dark metal rod connected to a monitor was set up next to the table. The technician turned the monitor toward herself, away from my mother and me and then ran the rod over my belly in small, circular motions.

Mom held my hand, and we locked eyes. I was glad I couldn't see the monitor screen. I think my mom was, too.

"Looks like five weeks, maybe five and a half," the technician said. "You're fine for a medical." She marked something on the chart we'd been given at the front office and released us back to Helen.

Mom took my hand; my sweaty palm gripped her paper-dry one.

Helen smiled at us. "Are we doing OK?" The fluorescent lights on the ceiling above us reflected small flecks of dust on the lenses of Helen's red glasses.

I wasn't sure at all that I was okay, but nodded yes anyway.

Helen led us to a different room and another kind face. She introduced us to Nancy, and I let go of Mom's hand to shake hers.

A full-color chart on the wall behind Nancy's desk displayed the insides of a woman's body: uterus, ovaries, digestive organs, arteries, veins, everything.

I imagined all those working parts inside of me.

Nancy wore a light blue lab coat with a plastic name tag pinned to the pocket. She leaned against the edge of her desk and glanced at my file. "According to your ultrasound, you meet the criteria required for a medical abortion. Do you understand what that means, Kara? Medical abortion?"

"Um. I'm not sure. Is that RU-486? My friend told me a little about that, but I don't really know much."

"Her best friend is apparently quite the activist," Mom said. "She seems to know more about this than either of us."

"OK. First, I'll tell you about Mifeprex, which is the brand name for the drug mifepristone in the U.S. It's called RU-486 in Europe. Here's a printout of everything for you to take home."

She handed me a piece of paper.

Frazzled nerves made it impossible for me to read or absorb one word. I scanned the page and handed it over to my mother.

"To keep a pregnancy going, a woman needs the hormone progesterone. Mifeprex is an anti-progestin. It works by binding to the progesterone receptors in a woman's body and blocking them. Without progesterone, the lining of the uterus breaks down and sheds, the same way it does when you get your monthly period." Nancy shook her head, she was silent for a moment. "Accurate information about reproductive health services has been suppressed. Women and girls have to seek out the truth for themselves, and proactively exercise their choices in spite of what they may hear via the grapevine or the Internet." She smiled, "You are lucky that your friend is one of those girls."

"I know," I said and felt really lucky to have Mel for a friend.

"At this stage, the embryo survives on what is called a yolk sac." Nancy's eyes were alert, a really pretty sea green. "Without progesterone, the embryo won't be able to implant and will shed with the rest of the uterine lining." I looked on the chart for the uterus and imagined a tiny sac floating in mine.

"One thing that really worries me," Mom said, "is whether Kara will be able to conceive normally after this. Will it negatively affect her fertility? I saw something about that online."

I put my head down, embarrassed. My mother glanced at me, her tone was soft and careful. "You may really want to have a baby someday, honey, you know?"

I nodded, but I couldn't let myself think about that. Not now. But part of me did want to know Nancy's answer.

"A lot of misinformation is out there, not only about Mifeprex, but about surgical abortion, Plan B, and birth control. False and unfounded information—that it causes cancer, sterility, even death—is put out there on the Internet by various organizations. The truth is that when administered properly, in a licensed facility with doctors and trained clinicians, it's completely safe ... but, make no mistake," Nancy looked at me, "this is not something a girl should buy over the Internet and take on her own, anymore than one should buy tranquilizers, birth control, or other medications without knowing the source. I would advise against that."

Mom nodded, she looked tired. She and my father had been scouring the Internet for information half the night. I was glued to TV sitcom reruns, trying to drown out their worried comments but overhearing them anyway: "Oh my. Bill ... look at this. That's scary. What do you think?" "I think you're looking at the wrong kinds of sites. Try Googling RU-486. ... OK, open that one, the fourth one down."

Nancy pulled me back to the present and continued, "Well, here are the facts: Mifeprex has been FDA approved since 2002 in all fifty states, and women have been safely using these drugs to stop unwanted pregnancies in France, England, and other countries for well over a decade. The truth is, we have more than three million unplanned pregnancies in the U.S. each year. I don't know what's going to happen if..."

Nancy stopped herself mid-sentence. She was frustrated, the way Mel gets sometimes. "I'm sorry. It's just that I see so much working here. You can't imagine."

My mother glanced down at the fact sheet in her lap, a slight blush crept over her face.

"I understand," Mom said in a whispery voice. Was she thinking about Statler or the picketing and harassment that the DLA had done in front of this clinic? The flyers? I was sure I'd never know.

My mother gave Nancy a half-smile and a nod. I regretted every envelope I'd stuffed and sealed. I wondered if my mother did, too.

"So, Kara, any questions?" Nancy asked.

"Um, so it will be just like my period? Cramps and then the bleeding starts?"

"Some experience heavier bleeding and cramping than a normal period; there may possibly be nausea, too. You can take ibuprofen for the pain, or acetaminophen. No aspirin. I'll want you to start these antibiotics with your dinner tonight." Nancy handed me a small plastic bottle.

I nodded.

"We'll give you a dose of Mifeprex now, and then you'll take another at home. All the instructions are on your fact sheet." She looked at my mother, "It may be a good idea to keep her home from school tomorrow; let her rest."

"Absolutely," Mom agreed.

"In a week to ten days, after the bleeding stops, we'd like to see Kara back here for a complete check to make sure that everything is OK."

"All right." My mother nodded.

Nancy's focus stayed on me. "Afterward, if you'd like, Helen can make you an appointment for counseling, Kara. Hallie, our counselor, is great and runs several support groups, too."

"Does that sound good?" Mom touched my knee.

"I don't know, I'm not sure."

"Well. Anything else?" Nancy asked us both.

My mother and I shook our heads.

Nancy handed me a small plastic cup and a glass of water. There was a pill in the cup. I'd wanted this since Mel had told me about it, but now I felt strange and scared and hesitant. The pill was small, harmless looking, just lying at the bottom of the plastic cup. But I knew it was potent, and final.

"What about pain. Can it feel pain?"

"No. An embryo has no developed nervous system or brain function."

"Is there something wrong, honey?" Mom asked. She seemed as scared as I was, maybe more. "Kara? Have you changed your mind?"

"No. I ... I don't know."

I stood there holding the pill and the cup of water. I glanced up at the wall chart, the full-color organs, and thought about my uterus, the tiny yolk sac.

"From everything we've just heard it seems pretty safe," Mom said. "I mean, unless you think you want to go through with the pregnancy, this is probably our best option."

A nervous giggle popped out of my mouth. Alice in Wonderland came to mind, all that happened to her from taking one little pill.

"What? Are you unsure about this, Kara? Talk to me. No matter what you decide, I'm with you. I love you."

I was sure, but I was scared, too. Really scared. I put the pill into my mouth and swallowed. I chased it down with a gulp of water.

"It's going to be all right, sweetie. You'll be OK." My mother hugged me. Her voice was a half-sure whisper.

"Can we not talk right now? Please?"

Mom nodded, she kept her arm around me while I gave Nancy the empty plastic cup. Nancy put a gentle hand on my shoulder.

I stared at the floor, too embarrassed to cry in front of her. Nancy took my hand, and I lifted my face to look at her. "Kara, I know this is hard. Please understand that no matter what you may have heard or read, this isn't an easy choice for a woman to make, at any age, but I'm really glad that you came to us for help when you needed it."

"OK," I said, quiet and shy.

"Please take these in five hours." Nancy handed me a sheet of instructions and the second dose in a tiny manila envelope. She stapled her card at the top of the instruction sheet. "And please call the clinic if you have any concerns or questions."

I gave a wordless nod, feeling as if I'd swallowed a ticking bomb.

We thanked Nancy and left her office. My mother and I walked back down the long hallway and out of the clinic without a word.

Back in the car, I took in a long, deep breath and let it whoosh out of me.

"I didn't know it would be so hard, Mom, you know? So scary. It kind of felt like I was jumping off of a cliff or something."

Mom was quiet, eyes staring blankly out the windshield. She had her hand on the ignition key but she wasn't turning it. "Sometimes," she said softly, "we plan to do something, and it sounds good in the abstract, but then the reality is different or more difficult than we thought. Sometimes we have to shift our thinking entirely. Our life just takes an unforeseen turn, you know? Nothing like what we'd planned at all." Mom started the car, lost in her own thoughts. It seemed like she was talking more to herself than to me. We pulled out of the parking lot and headed toward home.

Relief, stress, and confusion coursed through me. Without warning, I began to laugh and cry, both at the same time, a gush of tears, then little laughs escaping from my mouth like hiccups. My body took on a life of its own. I felt crazy and frightened. I clamped my hands hard over my mouth.

Mom pulled the car over and parked. She handed me the whole packet of tissues and put her hand on my arm. "Taking responsibility can be really hard."

"No kidding," I said, wiping my eyes.

"Adults don't always have such an easy time with it either, honey. When I think about some of the choices I've made … well. No one is perfect, that's all I can say."

A few minutes passed. My mother and I sat in the car, the two of us, just breathing and not saying a word.

"Ready to go now?" she asked. I nodded, and we pulled back out into the street.

I opened my window halfway. The sun was out, and the cool, fresh air blew across my forehead, calming me. Some of the same neighborhoods and streets we always passed on the Saint U's bus flew by.

I'd thought my parents would never forgive me.

But they had. Not only forgiven me, they'd held me up every step of the way. They'd broken their own rules, gone against everything they'd been taught to believe. For me. All they wanted was for me to be OK.

My parents really loved me. I knew that now. But what if *I* didn't love me? What if I couldn't forgive myself? Not knowing that was the hardest part, and still churning around inside of me as we turned into the alley and pulled up to our garage.

My mother and I had barely set our purses down when she started to take ingredients out of the pantry and set them on the counter. She was going to bake, a sure sign she was nervous. When I was nervous, my stomach gurgled, but my mother baked.

I took my Shakespeare book from my backpack and went into the living room. I curled up on the sofa, determined to conquer *Hamlet*, at least the first half.

The grandfather clock was ticking, its pendulum swinging. Time crawled. The minutes crept along toward the time when I'd need to take the second dose.

Mom entered the living room, twisting her hair up onto her head with a clip. Sweet, warm smells followed her, the scent of chocolate chip cookies with pecans baking in the oven. My favorite.

"Suddenly chocolate chip cookies seemed imperative," Mom said. "How're you feeling? Want some milk or tea? Anything?"

Mom flopped down next to me on the sofa. "Still trying to get through *Hamlet*, huh?"

"Yeah, it's been hard to make any of it stick, you know? Stress."

"Well," Mom said, and then she sighed, "I wish you'd told me sooner, honey. That you'd felt safe coming to me right away."

"Me, too. Before this happened would have been even better. I'm sorry, but I just couldn't, Mom."

"I'm sorry, too. I feel especially awful about the not feeling safe part, that you felt you had to sneak. I know I had something to do with that." My mother hesitated, stopping herself.

"What?" I asked, not understanding.

"Well, remember when Nancy said going to the clinic was hard for everyone? That making that choice was never easy?"

"Yeah."

She paused, gathering her thoughts. I waited.

"Well, years ago, before you were born, I'd been trying to have a baby for a long time. I'd had so many miscarriages I was afraid I'd never be able to carry a child."

"Jeez, I never knew that. How many?"

"Five." She said, "No, six. There were six in all. Each miscarriage was such a terrible loss, and every time I felt that I'd failed, that I was being punished for some reason I couldn't understand." She paused, took a breath, and continued. "So, I was almost forty-two by the time I got pregnant with you, and I was terrified that I might lose you, too. The doctor told me to stay in bed for the last three months of the pregnancy."

"Wow, three whole months?"

"Yes, and I would have done all nine if I'd needed to." Mom picked up a lock of my hair and let it drift through her fingers. "I really wanted you, Kara, so, so much. These last fifteen years of being your mother have brought me so much joy. More than you could ever know." My mother looked out the living room window, her gaze far away and sad. I was quiet, wanting to hear more.

"I found myself wondering today at the clinic, what would it feel like to be pregnant and *not* want to be? To dread waking up each day? And I realized something. I have never once tried to imagine that before today." My mother's eyes closed on her tears, holding them in. "I sat in Nancy's office, thinking about how judgmental I've been, how completely biased about this. I was condemning women for choosing not to carry their pregnancies to term, partly because of my own difficult losses but also because of the beliefs with which I was raised … the Church, my schooling, all of that. I really thought I was doing the right thing by supporting Bruce Statler's campaign, even though I had my doubts about him as a person at times. Can you understand that at all?"

"Yes, I can."

Mom paused. "Maybe I was jealous about the ease with which other women could get pregnant and have babies. I'm not sure. I can see now that I never once considered all the different circumstances there could be, all the reasons why a woman might not want to be pregnant. How she might be unable to deal with having a baby, emotionally or financially. Even though I knew about your Aunt Sarah, I just didn't apply that ... didn't let it be real for me. I guess I judged her and the choices she'd made, too."

I touched her arm. "It's OK, Mom," I said softly.

"No. It isn't. My own daughter was scared and alone and unable to come to me for help."

"Mom, don't."

"No. How could you tell me? I've been so openly vocal and one-sided about abortion and unwanted pregnancy. In a real way I was sitting in judgment of you, too, without even realizing it. I made coming to me for help impossible. I set up the ultimate roadblock."

A few tears escaped the corners of my mother's eyes, and she wiped them away. I didn't know what to say to comfort her.

"Oh, honey, I feel just awful that you had to sneak around, that you were in trouble and afraid. That home felt like jail. I know we've been too strict, overly protective." Her voice cracked. "I do, and so does your dad."

My mother hugged me, and I melted into it. I wanted to stay in her hug forever.

"The three of us, you, me, and your dad, we have to be able to trust one another. I want us to from now on. I really want that, Kara. More than anything."

"Me, too. I do."

We sat on the sofa for a long moment. The only sound was that of the pendulum on the grandfather clock moving back and forth—click-click, click-click. We sat like that until the loud buzz of the kitchen timer disrupted our peaceful silence.

"Oh!" Mom cried. "The cookies!"

We jumped up and ran down the hall in tandem.

In the kitchen, we alternated tasks. I pulled open the oven door. Mom picked up a potholder from the counter and slid the oven rack out. I grabbed a spatula from the drawer and lifted the edge of one cookie off the baking tin. They were just right, not too crispy and perfectly browned, without a trace of black on the bottom.

"Cookie perfection, I'd say."

We shared a smile.

My mother opened the refrigerator. "Milk?"

"Yes, please." I lifted the cookies one by one onto a plate.

We sat down on either side of the nook with two glasses of milk and a plate of warm cookies between us. I'd never felt closer to her.

It's Working

The bleeding started soon after I took the second dose. There were some twinges just below my stomach, a bad headache, and some cramps, but it was less pain than I'd expected. Not much different from a normal period. But it was more than that, and I knew it. I felt part relief, part sadness, part emptiness and aching deep down in the pit of my soul.

It was over. What had I done? *I'm sorry*, I thought, *so sorry*.

I took a pad out of the box under my bathroom sink and put it on.

"Mom? Mom?" I called downstairs. I heard my mother taking the steps two at a time until she was there, standing in the doorway of my bathroom. Concern washed over her, spread through her, and reached out for me.

"It's working," I said.

Mom hugged me hard and rocked me against her chest. She touched my cheek and wiped her eyes. "Oh, sweetie," she said softly.

"Why don't you take it easy, lie down for a while. Want some ibuprofen?" My mother took the bottle of pills out of my medicine cabinet and gave me two. "I'll make you some tea," she said.

I swallowed them and got into bed. My mother pulled my quilt over me, kissed my forehead, and said, "I love you, Kara." Then she closed my bedroom door quietly behind her.

I ran my fingers over my bedpost and touched Grandma's rosary. My eyes filled. A silent stream spilled down my cheeks and plopped onto my pillow.

Staring at my ceiling, I tried to picture myself remembering this moment, years from now, and being OK with it. I tried to visualize a grown-up me thinking back on this day as no big deal.

But I couldn't. It *was* a big deal. No doubt. Bigger than I'd ever allowed myself to imagine.

The house was quiet. The teakettle whistled in the kitchen. I could hear Mom taking a mug from the cupboard, a spoon from the drawer, and the tea tray down from the high shelf in the pantry.

After knocking on my door, my mother entered my room carrying the tray with the tea in the little blue pot, a cloth napkin, and a few cookies on a fancy china plate; she set the tray on my night table and sat down on the edge of my bed. "Let's call your dad at his office." She reached for my phone. "He'll want to know that everything's all right."

"Can you call him in a little while? I don't feel like talking right now."

"OK." Mom put the phone down.

"Stay with me for a minute, OK?"

Mom took my hand. "Sure, sweetie." She glanced at my bedpost. "Oh, Grandma's rosary. I hadn't noticed it hanging there." She ran her fingers over the beads and said, "I still miss her. So much."

I lifted the rosary from the bedpost, put it under my pillow, and sank my head into the downy softness, "Me too," I said. "I think about her a lot."

I squeezed my mother's hand and shut my eyes.

When I woke, the shades in my room were half drawn. Snow was falling. Steady, gentle flakes were drifting down to earth without a trace of wind.

The tea tray sat on my night table.

I put my hand over my stomach and sighed. I was going to be OK. I could hardly believe it.

Knuckles rapped gently on my bedroom door.

"Mom?"

My door opened a crack. "It's me, Dad. Can I come in?"

"Sure." I pushed myself up and leaned on one elbow, facing him. He was home early.

"Hey. How're you doing, Kariboo?" The last time he'd called me that I was in the second grade. He stood hesitantly in the doorway.

"I'm OK." I moved over, making room for him to sit down on the side of my bed. He walked in. "Your mom called me. Been sleeping?"

"Yeah. Guess I was really out."

He sat down next to me. I put my head back down on my pillow, curled my knees up, and tucked my hands under my face.

"Sorry, I don't know why I'm still so sleepy." I shut my eyes, unable to keep them open.

Dad stroked my hair with the flat of his hand. It felt nice. "That's OK, honey. We don't have to talk, and dinner won't be ready for another hour or so. I just wanted to check in on you and let you know I was home."

My father pulled the edge of my quilt over my shoulder; the bed creaked when he stood. He stopped by my door. I could sense him standing there, watching me. I opened my eyes.

"Love you," he said.

Part of me wanted to jump from the bed and run to him, to hug him and tell him there'd be no more secrets or lies. No more hiding. But I couldn't; I was too exhausted.

A small smile darted across my lips. "Thank you, Dad, for everything."

My father nodded, shutting my door softly behind him.

I took a long, deep breath into my lungs and let it out. It was OK to smile. OK to feel. I lay in my warm bed with the snow falling outside and listened to the soothing noises downstairs. My parents were in the kitchen making dinner and talking.

A peaceful feeling settled over me and ran through me. I let myself relax into it and closed my eyes.

Back on the Bus

Iris smiled at me, like always. She had no idea that a new version of me climbed up the bus stairs, a different me.

I searched the rows of seats. Mel's frantic wave rose above the sea of heads. The bus jerked forward, and I grabbed a hand-hold. Bump, sway, bump, sway. I navigated my way down the aisle. When the bus stopped, I dropped down next to Mel.

"It worked," I said.

"Oh, thank God. I was so worried when I didn't hear from you. I thought maybe …"

"Sorry, Mel, but I couldn't call or e-mail. Not even you. I kind of needed to hibernate, you know?"

"That's OK." Mel seemed hurt, like I'd blown her off. "Is everything, I mean, you're all …?"

"Yeah, totally."

Mel nodded. "That's great." She stared out the bus window for a block or two, fingering the zipper on the CD compartment of her backpack.

My down-the-aisle view was full of ponytails, head bands, and loose buns held with claw clips. A bunch of uniformed girls were on their way to another boring Saint U's day, and so was I. A small sigh of relief and happiness leaked out of me. Like that girl in the clinic waiting room had said, "One big phew for me." I smiled to myself, knowing exactly what she'd meant.

Life would begin for me again. For the first time in forever, I could feel that. Know that. A part of me felt bad for feeling so good; I was confused and just plain sad even though I felt so relieved that it was all behind me.

Mel turned from the window. "I know we'll go to our graves with this one, Kara, but part of me wishes we could just tell the whole world. It worked, you know? It's so awesome."

"Yeah," I said. "But it's weird. Like, one day you're in the worst trouble ever and then, bam, within a few hours, you have your life back."

Part of me did want to tell, but another, a much bigger part, didn't want anyone to find out. Ever. Mel and I were quiet until the bus pulled into Saint U's.

The thing was that everything felt changed for me, completely different. Mel had no idea, and I had no way to explain it to her.

When Mel and I got to homeroom, Evil Elaine was holding the front page of the *Denver Post* aloft, turning it face out to the class and moving it back and forth for everyone to see.

Sister was red-faced; her thin lips were pinched in a snarl. "This is an outrage!" Spit flew out onto the doomed front-row sitters.

"That right-to-die case. Here we go," Mel rolled her eyes at me as we took our seats.

It had been in all the papers and on TV the few days I'd been home, a story about a brain-injured woman in Florida who had been in a coma and unresponsive for quite a while, still breathing, but not really living. Her husband had ordered her feeding tube removed.

"This poor woman, a Catholic woman, is being starved to death. Starved! Christians and Catholics from every state have gone to Florida to hold a vigil for her. The pope is getting involved."

Mel gave me a sidelong glance, the ultimate sneer settled over her face.

Samantha raised her hand.

"My two aunts—they're from Connecticut—are down there right now."

A smile bloomed on Sister Elaine's face, and her full-throttle fury eased off a touch. "God bless them."

Mel groaned, waving her raised hand in the air. Sister ignored her, so Mel called out, "How can anybody really know what *she* wants when she can't even talk? She's brain-dead."

"Her parents say she's not. God knows. He knows everything. She wants to live, to hold on to life. The Lord will take her when He is ready," Sister Elaine replied.

Mel was surprised to see my hand go up. "But what if she *did* tell her husband that she didn't want to be kept alive artificially?" I asked. "Maybe this is not something for God to decide."

"Go back and study your Baltimore Catechism, Miss MacNeill. The most basic tenets of your faith are there. God is everywhere, and He knows everything," Sister Elaine shot back.

"How dare you blaspheme!" Mel snorted, under her breath.

In half a flash, Sister Elaine had swooshed between two rows of desks and was standing in front of Mel's. "What was that, Melanie?"

Mel sat up straight but gave no reply.

"What is your preference, Melanie—to repeat that to the entire class right now or to take a detention?"

Mel remained mute, defiant.

"It was nothing, Sister." My voice was calm and firm. "It's just that, Mel and I…"

Sister loomed over me, seething with rage and indignation.

I lifted my shoulders. "Um, we just don't agree with you. Our opinions differ, that's all."

"Well!" Sister spat the word out through her clenched teeth.

Mel used the sleeve of her blazer to wipe some spit from the tip of her nose. We didn't dare look at each another.

The bell rang. A flurry of books slapping shut, desk chairs being pulled back, and metal chair legs scraping across the linoleum tiles began.

Then everything stopped. Total silence. Everyone froze. Sister Elaine's eyes shot from Mel to me and back again.

The hallway was noisy with girls rushing to class and the opening and slamming of locker doors. Sister turned and faced the room of statue-still girls. Twenty-three pairs of eyes roved between Mel and me, the fate awaiting us, and the seconds ticking by on the classroom clock.

Evil Elaine turned on me, staring me down with her crazy mad intensity. I met her gaze and matched it, fearless. After almost a full minute, something in Evil Elaine surrendered; her rage seemed to melt before our eyes. She turned to the class. "Girls, didn't anyone hear the bell? Go now. All of you. You'll be late for your classes."

The startled girls vacated the room in seconds.

After we left the classroom, Mel pulled me over under the portrait of Saint Ursula. "That was so awesome! Incredible!"

Dakota flew past us, put her hand out to slap me five, and called, "Way to go!"

"Thanks," I called after her.

Mel and I hustled toward our classes, our best-friend status unquestionably intact, as if I'd never mangled it. As if Jake hadn't happened.

The second-class bell rang. I rushed into English class and took my seat, feeling different but in a really good way.

Friends and Enemies

The first time I walked into church after the abortion, I thought God might strike me down right there, in the center aisle, a big red A appearing on my blue dress for everyone to see, or maybe an M for "mortal sin." But nothing happened.

The same gray walls and beamed cathedral ceilings, the same gray wood pews and padded kneelers, the same martyred saints set in stained glass casting shafts of rainbow light upon the congregation surrounded me as I walked in and took a seat with my parents. Larry and Mary were sitting one row ahead of us. They smiled and nodded when we sat down. Mel, Sherry, and Troy were two rows behind us. The Moriarity family was sitting in the same row as we were, but across the aisle.

Sermon time. When Father Miller stepped up to the pulpit, I was wide awake.

"Right to die? Isn't that just a euphemism for murder?" Father Miller's angry eyes probed the congregation as if he was waiting for an answer to his rhetorical question. None came. "Yes, we're all going to move on at some point, go back to our Father in Heaven. But has it now become our decision to say when and where?" He shook his head and chuckled softly. "Well, as long as innocent babies are disposable, why not throw in some spouses along the way? What does it matter? It's only *life*."

Father Miller's piercing look discharged shame throughout the church. Many heads bowed, but not mine, and not Mel's. I glanced over at Larry and Mary—their heads were upright too.

"So, here we have a husband and wife, married in the Church, both of them raised Catholic, and he is asking that his wife's lifeline be taken away. He is asking them to pull the plug. To kill her! This is why the Holy See is getting involved, the president. Murder will be on this man's head. I tell you, he will burn in Hell for it."

The lecture continued, and I listened closely to his words. He brought Statler into it, told us how he was "our political voice, crying out in the darkness of current day immorality." He said that Statler should "shine his beacon" on the right-to-die issue, too.

I glanced at my mother. She was squeezing my dad's hand. They smiled a secret smile. Across the aisle, Mrs. Moriarity was nodding her approval. Emma winked at me as if we were connected, on some kind of winning team together. I looked back at the pulpit. *We're not*, I thought. *So not.*

I stayed alert for the entire sermon, and I thought about what Father had said—what I agreed with and what I didn't. I was hearing with new ears, seeing with new eyes. And I saw the families of the congregation in a new way, too. We were different people, with different viewpoints—all of us Catholic.

When it came time to shake hands and say "Peace be with you," Mary grabbed my hand in hers and looked me right in the eye. "Peace be with you, Kara," she said. "I hope all is well?"

I nodded. "It is, thanks."

A big smile lit up Mary's blue eyes. "I'm so glad to hear it."

The same crowd filed into the parking lot; the same rush for the cars took place. Dad put his key into the ignition and turned to me.

"What did you think, Kara?"

"About what …?"

"The sermon."

My father maneuvered his car past three others and made a left out of the parking lot, a smooth move.

"I don't think the Church should be involved with that poor woman or her family's decision. Not at all. I thought Father Miller was trying to force people to think his way, like he always does. Ugh. Did you see Larry's face?"

"Yes, and Mel looked ready to implode, didn't she?" Mom smiled. We all laughed.

"I think Larry and Mary take Father Miller's point of view with a grain of salt. They do their own thing," Dad said. "Worship in their own way."

We were all quiet with our own thoughts for a moment.

"Hey, maybe we could form our own branch of the Church with Sherry and Larry and Mary—whoever wants to join. One that's more like the end of *The DaVinci Code*, or *The Expected One*. Mel's all into that book now," I said, half-serious.

"Have you read *The DaVinci Code* or seen the movie? Wasn't it forbidden?" A tiny wrinkle formed in the middle of my mother's brow.

"No, but I'd like to. Mel's told me all about it. She's read the book, like, ten times. Dakota has too."

"Oh," my mother said. "Well, I suppose I did take a peek at it one day at Barnes and Noble. I thought it was a little far-fetched, but … who's to say?" She smiled at my father.

"So, we could take turns having services at one another's houses. Mom, you could say Mass from memory, right?" I leaned forward, on a roll, my hands gripping the backs of their seats. "And Dad, maybe you could hear confessions, or we could get rid of all the guilt trips and design our own thing. Something more esoteric and mystical. Mel says …"

My parents looked at each other and then gave sidelong glances back at me, eyebrows raised.

"Ha! Gotcha. Just a little creative thinking happening in the backseat," I said. It felt great just to talk, without having to second-guess their reactions or censor myself.

"Admirably innovative, I must admit," Dad said, with a grin. "Krispy Kreme, anyone?"

"Sounds mystical." Mom put her hand over mine and squeezed.

We laughed. My father changed the direction of our car, and off we went.

Telling, All of It

S oft peach colored walls, low lights, comfy sofas and chairs, more forms to sign.

Mom read a book while I flipped through a magazine, unable to concentrate.

"Kara? You can go in now."

My mother's eyes crinkled in a smile above the frames of her reading glasses. "I'll be right here," she said and settled back into the waiting room chair with her book.

A sign on the wall in the small counseling office read, "What we say here, stays here." I liked the face that greeted me. "Hi, Kara, my name is Hallie." Her hand felt warm in my cold one.

"Hi." I sat down, cleared my throat, and tried to get comfortable, but my mind was screaming: *Mistake, mistake!* I wasn't comfortable, not in the least.

"So, how does it feel to be back at school, getting on with your life? Big shift, huh?"

"I guess. Yeah." I exhaled way too loudly.

"So. What would you like to talk about today?"

A shy shrug from me. *Nothing*, I thought, *nothing*.

"How did your boyfriend react to your decision? Did you two discuss it?"

"He's not my boyfriend."

"Oh."

"Not my friend either."

Hallie's eyes were a deep, misty brown with dark, curly lashes.

"Would you like to tell me about him?"

There was no way. I lifted my shoulders, eyes trained on the window.

"Not really."

The day was sunny behind those closed blinds. I wanted to get up, open the blinds, and let the sun in. I wanted to fling the door open and run out of that room.

"Were you pretty serious about him?"

I lifted my shoulders again.

I guessed Hallie to be somewhere in her thirties. Her amber-colored shirt matched her eyes. I liked it and wanted to ask her where she'd bought it.

"We don't have to talk about him at all unless you want to, Kara." Hallie settled back in her chair, waiting me out.

There was a long, awkward silence. Hallie's eyes stayed on me, penetrating me. I felt like a chip of ice skittering across a hot griddle.

In less than a minute, I caved, unable to hold my silence. "We only went out a couple of times. A few parties, that's all. I thought he really liked me."

"OK," Hallie said. It was like she could see right through me.

"Then, I realized he didn't care about me at all. He's already with another girl."

"How was that for you, finding that out?"

"Bad. It really sucked."

Hallie sat for a minute, absorbing my words, her eyes told me that she really cared about what I was saying.

"What was his reaction to your pregnancy, Kara, when you first told him?"

"He was mad. He thought maybe I'd been with someone else."

"Oh. You mean he thought you'd had sex with other boys?"

I blinked back tears. "I guess. He asked me if I was sure it was his."

My knee was jiggling. Up and down, up and down. It wouldn't stop.

"But you hadn't had sex before? Before him, I mean."

I focused on my lap and my clenched hands. I shook my head no. "He was the first. For everything."

"I see. How old is he?"

"A senior. Eighteen."

"Did he ask you about birth control? Like, if you wanted to use a condom or if you were on the Pill?"

"No. He didn't." My hand was on my jumpy knee, pushing it down. I wanted it to stop. *Stop.*

"So, you'd planned to have sex that night, but you didn't think about birth control or being safe? Is that right?"

My heart was beating fast, too fast. Heat rose up on my throat and into my cheeks. I felt them turning pink, pinker. Hot and red.

"No. We were at this party, and I was pretty loaded. When he asked me to go upstairs with him, I thought we'd just make out some more and be alone, you know?"

Hallie moved forward in her seat. She rested her hands on the edge of it, listening hard. "Kara, did you want to have sex with this boy?"

Silence. I put on a blank, expressionless face and shrugged.

Hallie ignored the shield I was erecting around me, intent on piercing it. "What I'm asking is this: Was it a mutual decision? You both wanted to have sex, is that right?" Hallie's large eyes probed mine. She was on a research expedition, through my eyes and into my soul. "Kara?"

I looked away and then down. I didn't know I was crying until I saw a fat tear land on my clutched fist. I shook my head. "No, not really," I said, my face still down.

A pressure was building and building, inside of me. Something was coming up, coming out. Something I couldn't hold back.

Hallie handed me a tissue. I wiped my cheeks and blew my nose. Sadness covered my face. And shame. I looked up and let Hallie see that, let her see me.

"I'm sorry. I messed up. I shouldn't have had all those Jell-O shots. I was only trying to impress him and … I didn't want to look like a baby, a loser, you know? His friends were all older than me. I really thought I loved him."

"Did he force you, Kara?"

"No, I …"

"Rape is not your fault, you know. Never your fault."

Hallie's words fell like bricks all around me.

I sat up straighter and looked right into her full-moon eyes. "No. It wasn't like that. I said yes; I went upstairs with him. I snuck out … I wasn't even supposed to go out with boys. I should have stopped him. It was my fault."

Hallie eased back against her seat. "OK. Let's be really clear. Did you say yes to go upstairs with this boy or yes to having sex with him?" Her powerful eyes were intense, but her voice was soft and quiet. "Which was it, Kara?"

I rested my neck against the back of the sofa and turned my face up to the ceiling. "To go upstairs."

"That's not a yes to having sex, is it? That is not a yes to anything but going upstairs. Do you understand what I'm saying to you?"

Scrambled, mixed-up thoughts were bouncing all over my head. No, no, I had to stop. I couldn't tell.

"OK, yes, it does sound like you made some bad choices that night. Like sneaking out and binge drinking …"

I nodded. Hallie continued, "Maybe you put yourself in a vulnerable place by agreeing to go upstairs with him. But that did not give him the right to force sex on you, to rape you."

I stared at the floor, deep into the beige pile of the carpet.

"Am I wrong? Or is that what happened?" Hallie asked.

Without my permission, my head started bobbing up and down, up and down, all on its own … telling her yes.

"Does anyone know? Have you told your mother?"

"No, no one." My unsteady voice muffled the words.

Hallie sighed deeply. "Kara, you're a minor. I have to report this. Your parents need to be told."

Report it? To the police? My mind went crazy wild. Will they come over here and arrest me for underage drinking? Arrest Jake?

"NO! NO! NO!"

Was it me who was screaming? It didn't sound like me. I felt myself slipping off of the sofa and onto the floor, face down; my arms were folded over my stomach.

Hallie's arms were around my back, holding me. "Kara, you're fifteen. You've had non-consensual sex. By law, I'm obligated to report that."

My hands went over my ears, covering them, blocking her words out. I pressed my head down on top of my knees. The beige carpet was so close; I smelled chemical odors, it was new.

Hallie rubbed my back. "Kara? Come on, breathe, OK? Breathe."

No, not OK. Never OK again.

There was a knock on the office door, and the knob clicked open. A pair of brown loafers stepped onto the carpet. "Need help?" I recognized Helen's voice.

"Can you please ask Kara's mother to come in?" Hallie asked.

I was still on the floor, unable to move. Hallie's face was near my ear. She whispered, "We'll tell her together, all right?"

"Her mother's right here," Helen said. My mother's black flats entered the room.

I looked up and saw Mom's snow white fingers, her hands grasping her purse so tight she was cutting off the blood flow. Her darting eyes flitted back and forth from me to Hallie and back to me. My jaw clenched. I covered my face with my hands.

"Kara? Honey, what happened?" Mom crouched down on the floor beside me.

"Hi, I'm Hallie."

"Maggie," Mom said. They shook hands over me.

"Please have a seat, Maggie."

Hallie helped me up, and suddenly I was sitting on the sofa. But I didn't know how; I didn't feel my legs or body get me there. Hallie was next to me, and my mother was sitting on the bleached wood coffee table, our knees touching.

Mom took my hand.

"Mom, I ..." My mouth opened and then shut. Nothing more would come.

"You can tell her, Kara; it's OK," Hallie said softly.

Then the words gushed out of me, rapid-fire. "There was a party, and I snuck out to go with him, you know? I never meant to ... to have sex. He sort of, he just ... I didn't mean for it to happen, Mom. I promise I didn't. I tried to tell him to stop, but I couldn't. I tried, I ..."

Mom was squeezing my hand so hard that it hurt. Her eyes filled. "Oh, Kara. No." My mother's eyes searched Hallie's face. "She was raped? Oh God, oh no. That can't be."

"I'm so sorry," Hallie said gently.

Mom put her arms around me, and my heart split open with sobs.

"Shhh. Baby, it's not your fault. Shhhh," Mom said.

"I'm sorry, really sorry. I messed up so bad."

Hallie put a wad of tissues in my hand. "I'm mandated to report this, Maggie; Kara is under the age of consent. Please talk it over with your husband and decide how you want to proceed, whether you'll press charges."

Charges? Everyone would blame *me* if Jake went to jail. Everyone would hate me. My mind pulled away. From my mother, from Hallie, from the room. I was filled with one sure, silent thought: *NO!*

I'll Sue That SOB,
But What's His Name?

"**W**hat's his name, Kara? Tell me his name!"

This was the father I remembered, the one I had lived with all my life, the person who couldn't stand to lose. The lawyer guy.

"No, you'll press charges."

I was sitting barefoot on the leather chair in my father's home office, wearing flannel pajama pants and a faded Broncos T-shirt. Twenty minutes of a frustrating, no-win negotiation had already ticked by.

My father wiped a bead of sweat from his brow. A new tactic emerged, a smile, a softer voice.

"Sweetie, we've gone over and over this. You're a minor, and he's eighteen, of legal age. He broke the law, and someone needs to hold him accountable. We do. If we don't report him and he hurts another girl … "

"He won't, Dad." I interrupted. "I know it."

My father stood next to his desk searching his brain for another angle. He had a lawyer's brain, the instinct to push until he won, to make things right. His version of right.

My stomach growled. Tap. Tap. Tap. The heel of my bobbing foot slapped the dark wood floor.

"Will you please stop that?" Dad said. I stopped and looked at him. We were both nervous and upset.

"I made bad choices. OK? I know that didn't give him any right; I understand totally. But I snuck out, I drank too much, and there were consequences. A life lesson, like you always talk about. Now I've learned one. The hard way."

My father ran a hand through his hair. On top, where it had started to thin.

"So, you think that's fair? The guy just plain gets off?"

"Dad, you're always saying that life isn't fair." I stood up and crooked my neck to one side and then the other until it cracked. I sat on the window seat and swiveled my legs underneath me. "He didn't mean to hurt me, you know? He's gorgeous and popular. All the girls want to be with him. He assumed I did, too."

My father sank into his high-tech Aeron chair. He definitely didn't want to hear that; he hated to hear me say that.

"Well, you know what? That boy doesn't get to make assumptions about who wants what. I'm telling you, Kara, if he gets away with it this time, he will do it again."

"He was drinking, everybody was, and stuff got out of control. It's over, and I don't want to get into some ugly courtroom scene … not with him. I just couldn't deal with it."

My father leaned across his desk, his hands clasped in front of him. "I'm talking about reporting him, making people aware. Making him accountable for what he's done. Kara, you're strong and you're smart, and I'd be right there with you. I don't understand how you can let this guy get away with date rape. Why are you protecting him?"

My eyes welled up. "You *don't* understand. I'm protecting myself, not him. Can't you see how humiliating it would be? To sit there and look him in the eye, to accuse him? Don't try to make me. Don't." I was holding my tears in, stuffing them down. Down.

My father didn't want to upset me, but he definitely wanted to convince me.

"Who said anything about facing him in court? Again, all I'm asking is that we *report* this. It feels wrong, very wrong, to let the bastard walk away," he said.

The attorney in my father wouldn't stop. Couldn't. I pulled a wadded up tissue from my pocket and dabbed at my eyes. "Please let it go, Dad. Please. For me?"

My father got up from his desk and walked over to the window seat; he sat down next to me and put his hand on my shin.

"Somebody has hurt you, Kara, and I want to hurt him. Kill him, for God's sake, with my bare hands! Can you at least understand that? See where I'm coming from for just a New York minute?"

I nodded. I could. I did. I'd felt my father's love for me more in the last few weeks than I had in years. A quiet minute passed between us.

"Your mom says you've started going to a support group."

"Yeah, Hallie's, the counselor from the clinic."

My father's hands rubbed the top of his spread knees. "Do you think it's helping?"

"Yeah, it is. I'll be OK, I promise."

My father's eyes glazed over; he was staring at the globe behind his glass-topped mahogany desk, thinking and thinking.

He turned to me. "All right," he said, "for now I'll let this pass. I have no choice without his name." My father's hand went through his hair again. I sensed his frustration, how tightly he was holding it in. "Down the line, though, if and when I find out who the SOB is … If I …"

He stopped, pointed a finger at me, and touched the tip of my nose with it.

"Let me go on record right now: What I want, what I'd *really* like, is to put that chump behind bars where he belongs. Nothing would make me happier."

Dad's eyes were moist, but he was smiling at me. I leaned over and gave him a bear hug.

"I love you too, Dad."

Off the Bus

Mel grabbed the bus rail with one hand and looped her backpack strap over her shoulder with the other. "Come on," she called. "Let's go … my house."

Without thinking I jumped off at Mel's stop, and we started down the sidewalk together.

"God, I've been dying to have you over so we could talk."

"About?"

"Jeez," Mel groaned. "Everything! The clinic, how RU-486 worked, how the thingy was that my mom set up for your parents at Larry and Mary's house. Aren't they cool?"

A twisting, pinching knot formed in my stomach. Mel was talking too fast, walking too fast. Her tone was too happy, too casual, too excited.

"Earth to Kara? Come on, I want to hear it all!" Mel was in high activism mode.

"You know, I have something else this afternoon. I can't come over. I totally forgot."

"Not even for a little while?"

"No."

"Oh, OK." Mel's step slowed.

I stopped walking and faced her. "It's like this, Mel. The whole thing was really intense, and I'm in a support group. That's what I'm doing today, OK?"

Mel backed off. "OK, cool. Processing is all good. My mother took me and Troy after my father died. It helped a lot, just talking about our feelings and all that."

"Wow. You never told me you guys went to therapy."

"I was embarrassed, I guess.. I didn't want anyone to know. I thought everyone would think I was sick or crazy or whatever. I know, total weirdness on my part. Oh well, I was only twelve, a sevie." Mel started walking again. I followed.

"It's been hard for me, Mel. You just don't know."

"Hard like your hormones go crazy afterward and stuff? I mean, you're the only person I know who's ever been inside of a clinic or had a relationship even—a 'woman of experience,' so to speak. It's so awesome."

She smiled like that was a major compliment but I felt like a spreadsheet of facts Mel wanted to download.

I stopped walking. "Well, maybe it doesn't feel so awesome to me. Did you ever think about that? What do you expect, that I'll just come over and spill my guts, give you all the inside dirt? Is that what you want?" I hadn't planned to say that or use a nasty tone in my voice.

Mel turned and faced me. "Jeez, what's your problem? I mean, I only wanted to know, like, what it was like, going to the clinic and all."

"Right. I'm not your experiment, Mel."

"No, you're my best friend." Mel turned away.

We were a block from her house. I turned my back and started off in the opposite direction toward my house. I heard Mel's shoes hitting the sidewalk hard, taking her farther away.

I got panicky and called after her, "Mel, I'm sorry. I do have group in an hour. I really do."

"Whatever." Mel shrugged, she kept moving.

"I'll call you later or something, OK?"

"Fine." Mel threw the word over her shoulder at me, cold. She didn't turn around.

"Sorry, I just can't …, I …." My voice faded to a whisper. Mel continued down the block, her back to me.

I slowed my pace, turned and headed for my house.

Mel had been there for me. She'd helped me figure everything out. What to do and where to go for help. I loved her for that and always would. But I didn't want her propping me up now or telling me how exciting and cool it was for women to make their own reproductive choices.

I needed time and space to sort things out for myself.

Getting Help

Yellow shafts of sunlight spilled into the room through the rain-spotted windows. No plaster saints to spy on me here, no crucifixes or nuns.

A worn oak shelf of self-help books sat in one corner. Hallie called it our lending library. Six metal folding chairs were set in a circle on the deep brown carpet. No, seven. One more than last week.

I wrote my name on the sign-in sheet for the third time.

It felt strange signing my name on one of the black lines underneath the words *Survivors of Sexual Violence Group*.

Phoebe signed in after me. Phoebe wore a bright orange top and indigo jeans tucked into black combat boots. Her dark, curly hair was piled in a knot on top of her head. Phoebe seemed kind of wild, but I liked her.

Hallie walked in. "Hi everyone. I'm glad to see you all. A new group member will be joining us this afternoon. She'll be here after she's finished her paperwork, and then we'll do our check-in."

I bent down to tie a loosened lace on my sneaker.

"Here she is. Everyone, this is Shawna."

I looked up from my shoes and saw the new girl. My face flushed. Our new group member was standing next to Hallie—Shawna, from Head Start.

"Hey, what's up?" Shawna said, more friendly than she'd ever been at Head Start.

We smiled.

"You two know each other?" Hallie asked.

"Sort of. She helps out at my kid's school sometimes," Shawna said.

"Are you OK being in group together?" Hallie looked first at me and then at Shawna.

"Yeah," I said. "No problem."

Maybe it would be strange to have someone from the SUCH program in this group, but I didn't want to hurt Shawna's feelings.

"OK with you, Shawna?"

"Sure, I don't care." Shawna shrugged.

"OK." Hallie pointed to the white board with words written in thick purple marker on the easel next to her. "These are the rules our group has agreed to," she said and read them out loud. "Confidentiality—what we say here, stays here. Respect, for ourselves and for one another. And good listening—don't interrupt."

Shawna stared at the words on the board.

"Can you agree to follow these rules, Shawna? Do you have any questions about them?" Hallie asked.

"No," Shawna said. She plopped down into the empty chair next to Hallie. "I'm OK with it."

Tiffany raised her hand. "I really like the first one about trusting each other."

"Yeah, it's not that way at my house," Janine said.

"It's important that every one of you feels safe here, that you all know what we say while we're here will definitely stay within this group."

Everyone nodded their consent.

"OK," Hallie began, "let's go around the circle, introduce ourselves, and do check-in. We check in by saying how we're feeling today, Shawna, and if you'd like to add anything about yourself or why you're here, you can. Phoebe, will you start?"

"OK. Hey, Shawna. Hey, everyone. I'm Phoebe. This week I'm feeling kinda jumpy. I don't know why for sure. Maybe 'cause finals are coming up. I'm a junior in high school. I'm in this group 'cause when I was eleven, I was raped by a friend of my older brother's. I only remembered it about a year ago. Um, I guess that's all."

"Thanks, Phoebe. Janine?"

Janine was the girl with the diamond nose stud and cropped, hot pink hair I'd met in the clinic waiting room. She'd recognized me when I first joined the support group. Janine had a tiny red heart tattoo on her left hand. She wore heavy eyeliner, and was dressed all in black, same as the last two times. Definitely a goth.

"I'm Janine. Sometimes my friends call me J-nine or just Nine. I feel pretty good today, all right. I'm nineteen, going to DU in the fall on an art scholarship. I'm cool with that."

Some of the other girls called out "All right" or "Go, girl!"

"Thanks, Janine, and that's so great about your scholarship. You must be really proud of that," Hallie said, nodding for me to go next.

"I'm Kara. So far I'm not talking too much here, but I'm really listening."

Hallie smiled. "Thank you, Kara. How are you feeling today? Do you know?"

I thought for a minute. "Kind of shy, I guess."

"Thanks," Hallie said. She turned to the group and said, "Our feelings are always changing, and however we're feeling is OK." She nodded for Tiffany to take her turn.

"Hi everyone, I'm Tiffany. This is my third time here, and I feel OK about this group; it's making me deal with stuff. I'm feeling, um, kinda weird today. Don't know why."

Like me, Tiffany was new, and she rarely said anything in group. She wore short, zip-up boots, a long denim skirt, and big, sparkly earrings. Her strawberry blond hair was pulled back in a clip.

"Thanks, Tiffany. Brianna?"

Brianna always had that look, the kind you get when you find out there's a pop quiz and you had no clue.

"I'm Brianna. Today I feel kind of, um, I'm not sure."

Brianna was small and fragile with amber eyes and white-blond hair. Brianna was short on words, too.

"That's OK, Brianna. Sometimes we're just not sure what we're feeling. One of the reasons we're in this group is to connect more with our feelings and to learn to express them and be OK with them, whatever they are." Hallie leaned forward on her chair, her hands clasped in front of her; her deep brown eyes scanned the circle. "Hi everyone. I'm Hallie, and today I'm feeling glad that you're all here and that Shawna has joined our group."

Hallie's eyes stopped for a moment on each group member. I got the impression that she really cared about every single one of us.

"OK. Last week we talked about three words. Survivor. Sexual. Violence. These words are hard to hear, hard to say, and hard for a lot of girls even to think about. Last week, some of you were willing to share feelings about your experiences with these words and the reasons why you are here. Some of you said it's been easier to stuff your feelings, to pretend these kinds of things always happen to other girls."

That was me, a silent girl, hurt in all of those ways and still unable to say them out loud.

Shawna raised her hand.

"Yes, Shawna?" Hallie said.

"Should I do the check-in thing now?"

Hallie nodded. "If you'd like to."

"OK then. I'm Shawna. I got raped, and I got me a kid out of it, a little boy. His name is Cole. He's three now. I didn't think abortion was right, y' know? My stepdad, he told me it was a mortal sin. He said it was my fault anyhow, and I had to pay."

Shawna's jaw was set tight. She scanned the circle of faces, defiant.

"When it come to raisin' him, he don't help me none. He and my mom split up. I'm on my own with Cole. It's tough, y' know? I got two jobs, and I get real mad sometimes. I'm kind of afraid about that." Shawna bit her lip. She had no tears. "Anyhow, that's why I'm comin' here."

"That sounds hard, Shawna," Hallie said. "Your stepfather said you had to pay. Did he mean by having the baby, your son?"

Shawna's head moved up and down. She had no words.

Cole's little face popped into my mind, his sweet dark eyes.

"How do you feel about that?" Hallie asked Shawna.

"I feel mad. I can't help it. Sometimes I want Cole to just … hush."

"You mean, as if he wasn't there?"

Shawna thought about what Hallie had said and then nodded yes.

"It's hard to be so responsible for someone twenty-four/seven, isn't it?"

Shawna's eyes drifted up to the windows above us, to the fading beams of light, like she was finished. No one said anything, but there was a world of support in our silence.

"Sometimes Cole, um, he gets real mad, too. I love my son a whole lot. It's not his fault he got born; I know that." Shawna's blank eyes connected with no one. "My mom had her first baby when she was fifteen, too, my older brother. It didn't turn out too good for her to have us so young. She's been married three times now. Husbands don't seem to work out for her either."

Shawna sighed to herself. "I want to be a better mother than her; I got to be."

"Being a single mother is hard work at any age," Hallie said. "I believe you can do whatever you set your mind to, Shawna. Wanting to be a better mother is the first step. Realizing you need help and asking for it, like you're doing here, is the next."

Shawna glanced at Hallie and then away, out the window; her eyes were edged with tears.

Hallie offered the blue enamel tissue box, but Shawna shook her head no. I wished we could give Shawna a big, group hug, but I doubted she would let us.

Brianna raised her hand, and Hallie nodded for her to take her turn.

"Well, OK," Brianna exhaled heavily. "I'm here 'cause my older cousin messed with me when I was, like, ten. I was all confused, like, what's happening here? Then I felt real bad and thought everything was my fault and all." Her eyes browsed the group, taking in the looks of understanding and recognition from the other girls. "But now, after coming here? I'm starting to get that maybe it wasn't my fault." Brianna sat back with a satisfied smile. Finished.

Shawna and Brianna exchanged shy smiles. The group was silent for a long moment.

Janine shifted in her seat. "This guy I knew, he didn't wait. He didn't listen when I said 'No! Stop! Get off me!' The jerk, he just kept on, like I wasn't even there, y'know? He was like, yeah, oh yeah. Bam, bam, bam." Janine made a hammering motion with her fist, then used it to wipe a tear away. "But where was he when I turned up pregnant? Long gone. I never told my parents. Nobody."

A dull ache swept through me. I put my hand over my stomach.

Hallie passed the box of tissues to Janine. And I felt my mouth open, words gushed out, all on their own. "All he said to me was, 'Want to go upstairs?'" I could barely hear my own voice. "I didn't mean for it to happen."

Phoebe was sitting next to me. She turned in her seat. "That's right. He stole something from you, girlfriend."

"Yeah, they just stole it!" Janine called out. "It sucks!" She was mad.

Anger rose in my chest. Shame filled me. Janine wiped her tears and offered me some tissues; our sad smiles connected over the box.

"Deciding to drink is one choice. Deciding to have sex is a different choice," Hallie said.

I shifted in my chair. The metal hinges squeaked. "I drank. A lot. And I went upstairs with him."

"Maybe those weren't the best choices, Kara. That still didn't give him the right to rape you," Hallie said.

A chorus of yeahs and uh-huhs came from around our circle.

Rape. The word punched my heart. Jake had raped me. It was still hard for me to let that in or admit that I was too drunk to stop him. The two times I'd been to group, I'd kept quiet, afraid to expose myself, to speak the truth. Speak it out loud.

Phoebe's eyes searched mine. "OK, Kara. Suppose when you got upstairs he had asked you, 'Hey, want to have sex?' What would your answer have been?"

"Well, I'm not sure," I said. "I was pretty drunk."

"The you-can't-even-talk kind of drunk? Or the silly kind?" Phoebe wanted to know. Everybody laughed, even me.

"Yeah, I could talk."

"So, yes or no?" Phoebe persisted.

I acted like I was contemplating my response. I knew the answer, but I hated it.

"No." The word was a whisper at first. Then louder, "I'd have said no. Definitely. NO."

Phoebe's eyes cruised up to the ceiling and then came down. "All right then," she said, emphatic.

"We heard that, Kara, loud and clear. Good for you," Hallie said.

Shawna raised her hand, and Hallie nodded.

"But my stepfather, he said everybody always blames the boy. What about what we done, our part? He told me I acted like a slut and gave that boy the wrong idea," Shawna said.

"But how do *you* feel, Shawna? Do you agree with your stepfather? Do you blame yourself for being raped?"

Shawna wrung her hands in her lap and made them into fists. "Uh-huh, guess I do. I got told it so many times. And my mom, she took his side of things anyway." Her dark brown eyes had a storm behind them.

The room was still, all eyes on Hallie; her voice was very soft. "Well, I disagree. I don't think you were to blame."

"Yeah, no way!" Phoebe and Janine said at the same time.

"Men and boys are not supposed to guess whether or not a woman wants to have sex, whether or not she's using birth control. Not because of the way we're dressed, how much alcohol we drink, or if we choose to walk up a flight of stairs."

Hallie's intense eyes darted around the circle of girls.

"But wasn't it my fault if I was too drunk to shove him off, to see what was happening until it was too late? I didn't say no loud enough." I was crying then. Hard. I didn't care who saw me. I pulled some tissues from the box on the floor and wiped my eyes.

Silence, waiting. I felt every girl in the room right there with me; they weren't just watching me from the outside. Hallie was with me, too. Her eyes penetrated mine.

"Kara, getting drunk and putting yourself at risk was probably not a good idea. But, please, I'm asking you to take a look at his part, at his responsibility for what happened. Ask yourself why you're taking all the blame. You don't owe him that, and I think, deep down, you know it."

A white silence filled the room. Hallie's words applied to every one of us.

Hallie waited a minute and then continued. "It's not a perfect world. We all realize that. There are choices in life and there are consequences. We don't get several chances to make a good decision. Most of the time, we get only one shot. The goal is to try to make the best possible choice for ourselves in each circumstance in each moment."

Shawna leaned forward in her seat; her gaze skimmed the circle.

"Like me, choosin' to come here and trying to be a better mother to my boy." Shawna's voice broke. "Because I love him, a whole lot."

"Right, Shawna, and I know you're going to be successful," Hallie said. She reached over and put her hand on Shawna's shoulder.

Shawna smiled and then nodded at me, her eyes glassy with tears.

I'd been so intimidated by Shawna at Head Start. I'd had no clue who she was or what her life was about. I felt sorry for judging her.

Hallie flipped a piece of her dark, curly hair behind her ear. "So, you're all here because you've been hurt and victimized in some way. Of course, it would be great if bad things never happened, if we could go back in time and prevent them. But bad things did happen, they happened to each of you. So, how can you make something good come out of your difficult experience? For yourself?"

Clueless looks flew around the circle; Hallie's suggestion sounded impossible.

"I'm asking you to think about this over the next week, to try and see how the awful experience you've survived can help you to stretch and grow. Think about how it might create resources for you and levels of insight you may never have found otherwise."

All of us looked pretty doubtful about finding anything positive in our awful experiences.

"Always keep in mind that how we choose to see an event affects how we feel about it."

We looked around at one another. There was hope in the air, too. The group's faith in Hallie helped us trust. If we looked hard enough, maybe we'd find something of value. Maybe, maybe not, but it was worth a try.

"Remember that feelings always change. They're fluid. They don't stay the same unless we force them to. If we can deal honestly with our difficult feelings, we can move through them to the other side. I know it can be hard to see that when you're young, but I believe in all of you. I know how hard you're trying to help your-selves, and I admire each and every one of you for all the excellent work you're doing in our group each week. So thank you for really being here, and I'll see you all next time."

I left the building feeling really good about being in Hallie's group. Glad. I ran everything through my head while waiting for my mother to pick me up.

Stolen. Jake had stolen something from me. My sense of me, deep down, felt bad. Bruised, and ruined. The hardest thing seemed to be how to find me again, the me I'd lost the night of that party in Cherry Creek Village. That Kara had gone missing. She was so far away that I couldn't feel her anymore, even in my dreams.

Mom's Saab pulled into the parking lot. I opened the door and got in.

"How'd it go today?" My mother sounded casual, but I could tell she was worried about me.

I put my seatbelt on. "OK," I replied. "Better this week. Good."

"I'm glad." Mom smiled.

When we drove out of the parking lot, Shawna was standing at the bus stop. She waved and smiled, and I waved back.

"Who's that?" Mom asked, checking her rearview.

"Someone from the group," I said. "A friend."

A girl who's brave, I thought, *and strong. A survivor.*

I leaned back against the soft black leather seat, enjoying the warm spring afternoon, and had another thought.

Like me.

After dinner, I cleared the table, loaded the dishwasher, and turned it on. My parents had gone into the den to read.

I went up to my room to call Mel. She picked up on the first ring.

"Hey," I said, "sorry about today. You really helped me, Mel, you helped get me out of the worst trouble of my life."

"OK."

"I mean it. I'm just going through a tough time. The last thing I meant to do was hurt your feelings."

"I thought you'd need someone to talk to. Isn't that what best friends are for?"

We were silent a moment.

"Remember when you said you felt all weird about going to therapy after your father died?"

"Yeah, but, that was ..."

"That's how I feel now, weird, because a lot of stuff is coming up ... private stuff."

"O-*kay* then. My lips are zipped." Mel's tone was hurt, edgy.

"Don't be mad. I know you're really curious and all and that the whole pro-choice thing is huge for you, and I really appreciate how much you know about it and the way you helped me. But, jeez, Mel, I need time to figure some things out. And I need to figure them out in my own way."

"All right, I get that. You don't ever have to tell me anything unless you want to."

"It's not that," I said.

"Then what?"

"I just felt sort of pressured this afternoon, you know? Maybe it will be good to talk about everything sometime. But it has to be when I'm ready."

Mel let out a long breath. "Guess I did come on pretty strong, like a nosy reporter or something. Pushy me, sometimes I can't help myself. Most of the time, to be precise. Sorry."

We both laughed. I missed Mel, missed our closeness. I didn't want her mad at me.

"This much I am clear about. I was really glad when the drug first started to work, but I was also really sad, too. Both, at the same time."

"Yeah?"

"Yeah. Even though I was scared about being pregnant and the idea of having a baby, it felt so final. I didn't expect that."

"Wow. I guess I can't imagine. No way."

There was a pin-drop silence on both ends of the phone.

"Do you ever think about Jake?" Mel asked.

"Not if I can help it. That's been hard, too."

"Yeah. Well, never having had so much as a date, I'm slightly in the dark."

"From my perspective? Take your time."

"An expert opinion, I'd say."

A long silence. We could hear each other breathing.

"Well, I'd better go, get to the homework. I just wanted to apologize. Are we OK again?" I asked.

"One hundred percent," Mel said.

"We've got a Spanish quiz tomorrow, right?"

"Sí," Mel said. "Hasta mañana, mi amiga."

And we hung up.

Current Event

A platter of warm French toast and crispy bacon was waiting for me on the table in the nook. French toast for breakfast was almost as good as having a hamburger day at lunch time.

Mom poured coffee for herself and took a carton of half-and-half out of the fridge. "Morning, sweets. Sleep well?"

"Perfect. This looks great."

I loaded my plate and sat down.

Mom poured half-and-half into her coffee and stirred. The phone rang. Mom looked at the Caller ID and hesitated. A look passed over her face like she'd swallowed something bad. She picked it up.

"Hello? … Hi, Jean, OK … I know, sorry to have been so out of touch. … This afternoon?" Mom walked into the dining room with the phone but didn't lower her voice. "I'm sorry, Jean, but I can't. I know I said I would a while ago, and I feel awful for backing out, but … well, I've changed my mind, that's the truth of it."

Mom sat at the dining room table, wiggling her foot like mad and listening to Mrs. Moriarity. "Well, about everything, I suppose.

I just don't feel right being involved with DLA anymore. What? … Oh. No, it hasn't been sudden, not really. It's been happening over the last month or so. I've just had a change of heart, Jean, as simple as that sounds. I've missed meetings because I needed to sort things out for myself, to be sure. … Uh-huh, yes. I know. And I feel the same. I guess I should have spoken sooner, and I'm sorry for that. … Yes, all right. I see. We're in the middle of breakfast now, but maybe we can have tea sometime and talk? … OK, thanks. I am sorry, Jean. Bye."

Mom clicked the phone off and came back to the kitchen. She took her coffee cup from the counter and sat down across from me.

"Phew, that was hard."

"Was she mad?"

"More surprised than mad, I think. I've kind of avoided talking to her. I've missed meetings and made excuses. Avoidance is not exactly the best way to handle a situation. Guess I'm not being a very good role model, huh?"

I helped myself to more bacon. "Mom, you're a great role model. And a great cook, too." I smiled at her.

"I hope Jean and I can still be good neighbors, even if my quitting DLA means we can't be good friends."

"No secrets, no lies, right?"

"Absolutely. If I can't be myself around her then, well …"

"Maybe she wasn't really your friend anyway?"

Mom patted my hand and smiled. "Sounds just right." She glanced at her watch. "Better scoot or you'll miss your bus."

"Yeah." I got up and hugged her. "Love you, Mom."

"Thanks, sweetie. Have a great day."

My whole world seemed changed, rearranged. Moving along the sidewalk and passing the same houses, the same lawns, the same neighbors, I felt like a stranger to myself. Everything was the same, but it was different, too.

"Hey, Kara! Kara, wait up."

Emma Moriarity was huffing and puffing up the sidewalk half a block behind me. I was surprised to find myself stopping, actually waiting for her to catch up. Walking to the bus with Emma, or talking to her, didn't seem like such a big deal anymore.

"Hi, Emma, how's it going?"

"Good." Emma slowed down, out of breath. We continued walking for a minute. "Can I ask a question?"

"Sure."

"Is it, like, so cool once you get into the upper school? It seems awesome." Emma's seventh-grade self gazed up at me, full of innocence and curiosity.

"Yeah. Pretty cool," I said. "You have a lot more responsibility though."

"Like what?"

"Like everything. You start to grow up, be part of the world in a new way. You can learn to drive, and you can go out and do things on your own. You have choices to make, you know? It's important to try to make good ones for yourself."

Emma took this in, and smiled. "You sound like our life skills teacher."

We'd reached the curb. The bus groaned up the block toward us, brakes screeching.

"Well, upper school sounds fun anyway. I can't wait!"

Emma and I boarded the bus. I went to sit with Mel, and Emma joined her sevie clique up front.

There were other things I could have told Emma about upper school and about growing up in general. That lying and sneaking are relatively easy once you get the hang of it, but telling the truth and being yourself, that's hard. And choices? We make them every day without a second thought, or even a first. But Emma would have to find out the truth of things for herself, in her own way, and make her own choices.

"How's this for current events?" Mel asked, waving an article she'd clipped from the *Denver Post* in my face.

"Oh shit, current events today. I forgot." I collapsed onto the bus seat next to her. "Damn. My dad didn't bring the paper home yesterday."

"This was in this morning's paper. Maybe Evil won't call on you. She usually only has the time for three or four. Besides, she's afraid of you now." The thought made both of us grin. Mel slapped me five.

I leaned my head against the cold metal bar on the back of my seat. "Ugh. I hate current events, don't you? And global studies, what a total bore."

"This article is for your personal perusal, not for current events," Mel said, dropping it into my lap.

The bus lurched and stopped. Two more girls got on. The piece of newspaper drifted into the air and landed on the floor at my feet. I grabbed for it … my jaw dropped when I saw the headline.

"Yeah," Mel said. "He scores again, but not the basketball kind. No offense, but what a total loser."

"Wow. When did this happen? Is she pregnant?"

"Doesn't say. Long enough ago for her family to bring a lawsuit against the bastard. I hope the bozo loses his scholarship," Mel sneered. "I really do."

And then, "Whoa, he didn't do that to … " but Mel didn't finish her question.

I kept my eyes on the clipping as if I hadn't heard, and avoided Mel's stare. I could feel her penetrating eyes on me. Knowing Mel, she figured out the truth right then, but she kept quiet about it.

The words thudded through my heart as I read them: "*The senior star of the Cherry Creek High School basketball team has been arrested and charged with rape, according to the Denver chief of police. He claims innocence on all charges. His father called the allegations 'ludicrous' and said he will support his son …*"

"It doesn't give the girl's name or even where she goes to school," I said.

"Of course not. Jeez! Would you want people to know if it were you?" Mel asked.

My eyes stayed on the article. I wasn't going near that one.

"She's under eighteen, a minor." I was gripping the newsprint so tightly it almost ripped in two when our bus rocked over a pothole.

"Well, her name will probably get out if this goes to trial. Then everyone in Denver will know. Poor kid." Mel shook her head in solidarity.

I folded the clipping and tucked it into the front pocket of my backpack. "Thanks, Mel."

"No problemo," Mel said, heading down the bus steps.

My heartbeat pulsed in my throat as I walked off the bus. *No, no, please no*, I thought. *Don't let it be true.*

My morning classes went by in a haze. He had done it again, just as my father had predicted. The same thoughts kept spooling through my brain: I should have told. I should have told. My father was right.

I wished I had the choice to make again—to tell, to blame Jake instead of myself.

Bastard. Son of a bitch. Mel had him nailed from day one: arrogant asshole.

I thought about what we'd learned in group, how we got only one shot, how we should always be trying to make the best choice, trusting our feelings ... and how I kept taking responsibility for what Jake had done.

It was a hamburger day.

Maura and Jenna were already through the long line and headed toward our table with loaded trays. Mel and Dakota let me cut.

"Not really hungry," I said, grabbing a raspberry yogurt and some bottled water. I was too upset to eat. I left the line and the hamburgers behind me, and Dakota and Mel with question-mark eyes.

Maura chomped into her chile-and-cheese burger as I sat down. Green and yellow ooze was dripping out from either side of her bun.

"Yum," she said. "Hell for me would be a place without cheeseburgers."

"Hey, what's up?" Jenna asked, casing out my skimpy tray. "You're not doing South Beach or any dumb diet, are you? You're so skinny, no matter what you eat."

"No, I'm just not hungry."

"You can have some of my fries, if you want."

I scooted over so Mel and Dakota could slide in next to me.

Maura scooped a gob of ketchup onto a crispy fry. "Seems like your 'ex' is in deep shit."

"Oh yeah he is," Mel agreed, placing fat tomato slices on top of gooey yellow cheese and green chile.

"Good thing you broke it off," Dakota added, shoving her plate of fries toward me. "Want some?"

I declined the offer. Maura smirked and said nothing but only because her mouth was full. She was so easy to hate.

"Well, I feel really sorry for that girl, whoever she is," Mel frowned, carefully placing a crisp lettuce leaf on top of her tomato slices.

"Yeah," Jenna added. Then, "Why?"

"Because, like, who'd want to go up against that bastard in court? All of Cherry Creek High will find out where she lives and burn her house down or something."

"God, what if she *goes* there!" Jenna said.

"Doubt it. She probably goes to East High. For sure he's been through every girl at Cherry Creek by now. Then again, she might be a middle schooler. What a total lech." Maura's nasty eyes were mocking me.

"Why do you always have to be such a bitch?" I said. "You really piss me off."

Maura coughed, she almost choked. I opened my bottle of water, staring her down while I took a sip. She looked away, unable to meet the challenge in my eyes. An uncomfortable hush fell over our table.

Mel came to the rescue. "Can we please talk about something a little less revolting than Mr. Basketball? I'm trying to enjoy my lunch." Mel picked up her burger with both hands and turned it a time or two, searching for good first-bite placement.

Everyone was silent for a long minute, chewing and watching the drama unfold.

"OK?" Mel persisted, "Like, over and out, out of our minds, out of our little universe. Let's never mention the J word again. Am I right? He's so not worth our energy."

"Absolutely," I agreed, peeling the foil off the top of my yogurt.

"Yeah, basketball season is over soon, and so is he." Dakota smiled at me, on my side.

Jenna and Maura shrugged and nodded, reluctant to let go of all that great gossip potential.

"Whoever that girl is, let's hope she gets him good." Mel poked me with her elbow.

"Amen," Dakota agreed, and slapped Mel five.

School finally let out. I got on a different bus to take a different route—one that went downtown.

What if he wasn't there? He had to be.

Different restaurants and neighborhoods passed by, and different kids were on the bus—some sophomores, some freshman, and a scattering of middle schoolers. None of them were my friends. But that was OK because I wanted to be solo; I needed to do this alone, on my own.

Out the bus window I saw a poster. I saw the reflection of my face on the glass as "PRO-LIFE? CHOOSE STATLER, CHOOSE LIFE!" swept across it. A wry smile spread to the corners of my lips. I had chosen life. I chose to heal my life, to learn from my mistakes. To grow and change.

What living person was *anti*-life, I wondered. Living, breathing, alive, walking around on the earth—didn't that make a person pro-life? Yeah, I was happy, and sometimes sad; I was a whole mix of thoughts, feelings and desires. I was alive, and I was completely *for* it, to use another word—"pro."

Bruce Statler's campaign used the "pro-life" slogan to make people feel guilty, to make them feel wrong.

Being in Hallie's group had helped me to realize something. I wasn't going to find the old me; I was discovering the new one. I was putting her in charge.

Off the bus, one block from his building, I began to sprint, my backpack weighing me down. Breathe in, breathe out, breathe in. I was alive, and strong.

I reached the entrance to his office building and turned the worn brass knob of the heavy oak door.

"May I help you?" the woman at the reception desk asked. It was the first time I'd ever been to my father's office on my own. The receptionist didn't recognize me.

"Yes, please. Is Bill MacNeill in?"

"Hold on, I'll ring him."

I sat on one of the sofas in the waiting area and looked around me. Images of pueblos, ancient wooden gates, and adobe walls bordered with bright pink and white hollyhocks; dusty landscapes of mesas and mountains in muted browns, purples, and greens lined the walls of the lobby. The same artwork had been hanging here the day my mother brought me to this office. We were going out to lunch with my father for my tenth birthday. We had just bought the yellow flowered wallpaper for my bathroom.

"Excuse me, may I tell him who's calling?" The receptionist was covering the mouthpiece of the phone with her hand.

"Kara. MacNeill. I'm his daughter."

"Oh, hello! My, I didn't even recognize you!" She smiled and took her hand away from the phone. "It's your beautiful daughter, Mr. MacNeill. So grown up! Shall I send her up?"

She flashed me a big smile and motioned toward the elevators. "He's just finished with a client. Go right on up. Third floor."

"I know. Thanks."

I exited the elevator, walked down the green carpeted hallway and knocked on his door: William P. MacNeill, set in gold-leaf block letters, edged in black, on the frosted glass.

The door opened. "Hey! What a great surprise! Come in."

I realized just how glad I was to see him standing there.

"Oh, is everything all right? Did something happen at school?" My father's surprise had morphed into concern in a heartbeat.

"Everything's OK, Dad. I'm fine, really. Something has come up, though, and I wanted to talk to you about it, right away."

With bags under his eyes and a pimple germinating on his left cheekbone, my tired and sleep-deprived father motioned for me to sit down. He'd been making the long drive back and forth to Colorado Springs for the last several weeks, staying overnight in a hotel for several nights off and on while working on some big case. I felt bad for never even asking him what it was about or how it was going.

Dad eased himself onto the sofa, his eyes crinkling into a smile. "OK, shoot."

I dropped my hefty backpack to the floor and sank down into the dark brown leather chair across from him and reached into my backpack to retrieve the folded article.

"Been thinking about what you'd like for your birthday? I mean, besides driver's ed. You're all signed up for that. Your mom thought you might want to have Mel and some of the other girls spend the night?"

"Probably not. I'm not sure." I took the folded clipping out of the zippered top pocket.

"Or, your mother and I could take you out to dinner, some place elegant. Your choice. You could invite Mel and some other friends, too, if you'd like."

"That sounds kind of fun." I smiled. A few months ago, being seen in public with my parents would have equaled the ultimate in humiliation. Now, it seemed OK.

"Well, think it over and let us know."

"I will." I handed him the article, my insides churning.

My father scanned the piece of newsprint with blank, tired eyes, then looked up at me. "You know him?"

"Dad, you were right about him ..." I began.

Suddenly, my father got it; his eyes saucered. "Oh my God. *This* was the boy? The basketball star?"

I nodded yes.

My father read it over again, carefully, shaking his head, "Oh, Kara, wow. What do you think you want to do?" It was all right there, in front of him. He knew, and he was leaving it up to me. My choice.

I leaned forward, my elbow sank into the plush chair arm. "I'm not sure, Dad. I just know that I want to help her. Whatever that means, however I can."

"You mean you'd testify for the prosecution if this goes to trial? Tell them what happened to you, to help this girl?"

"Yes."

"He'll be in the courtroom, you know. Right there, in front of you."

I sat there, imagined that, then met my father's eyes, "I know. And I don't care." My voice was solid, certain.

My father sat back against the thick leather sofa and let the article fall into his lap. He let out a long sigh.

I watched him, aware that his brain was revving into high gear, that he was clicking through all the possibilities, probabilities, pros and cons of the situation.

"Kara, are you sure about this? There's a good chance your name will come out. The fact that you had an abortion even. Everything will be fair game."

"I know, Dad, and I've thought about that, too. All day, ever since Mel gave it to me on the bus this morning. Somehow, it just doesn't matter anymore, you know? If it comes out, I'll still be me. It wasn't my fault, not his part of it. I know that now."

I got up, moved over to the sofa, and sat down next to my father. "I'll be all right."

He looked so worried for me.

"Dad, I can do this."

My father tossed the article onto the coffee table in front of us and sighed again. He ran his thumb and forefinger across his closed eyes.

"But, I will need an attorney." I grinned. "You available?"

Dad clasped my hand in both of his; his eyes were steady on mine. "I think that can definitely be arranged," he said. "I'll be with you, Kara, every step of the way."

And I knew he would be. No doubt.

Reader's Guide

Kara doesn't understand why her parents are so strict, why her father has so many "ludicrous rules." Over the course of the book, do you feel her parents' protective ways hurt or help Kara? Give some examples to illustrate your answer.

Hiding the truth is a way of life for the members of Kara's family at the beginning of the novel. When Jake asks Kara to go out with him, she can see no way to accept without sneaking out and breaking her parents' rules. She says, "My parents could never know." Were there other ways Kara could have seen and gotten to know Jake without sneaking out and lying? Discuss.

While her friends are talking about reproductive rights and Catholicism, Kara realizes that she has no opinions because her head is "full of Jake." She is bored by her friends' cafeteria conversation, her school, and her life. Jake is all she can think about. Finding ways to talk to and be with him become her main focus. How does this line of thinking get in the way of Kara's making good choices for herself?

At one point in the novel, Kara refers to her father as "my jailer." How does her father change, and how does Kara's relationship with him transform by the end of the book?

How closely are Kara's thoughts about her actions related to the beliefs and values she's been exposed to through her religion and her parents? Do you think there is a transformation in Kara's thoughts and actions as a result of changes in her beliefs, or vice versa? How does the story show this?

Kara thinks Mel's negative comments about Jake are the result of jealousy. Do you agree? Why or why not?

When Kara reads one of the flyers for Bruce Statler's campaign, she thinks they are "Harsh. Much harsher than the ones I remembered the DLA sending out when I was eight." But Kara stuffs the envelopes as her mother asks her to without further thought or comment. Find other places in the novel where Kara doesn't listen to her own thoughts and feelings but instead goes along with what other people expect her to do. Discuss how Kara might have acted differently in those situations.

When Kara and Mel were in seventh grade, Mel's father was killed by a drunk driver. Kara and Mel vowed at his funeral never to drink alcohol. Kara breaks her vow for Jake, and later regrets it. How could she have answered Jake when he pushed her to drink at Rob's party? What did Kara learn at Hallie's support group that could have helped her deal with the pressures Jake put on her? Find places in the novel where characters respond to peer pressure and do things in order to look cool.

When Mel asks Kara to tell her about her experience at the clinic, Kara feels "like a spreadsheet of facts Mel wanted to download." Was Mel out of line? Do you think best friends always have to tell each other everything? Give some examples of situations to support your answer.

In the chapter After-School Snack, Mel asks Kara why she and Jake didn't use birth control or Plan B. Kara is relieved when she doesn't have to answer because they are interrupted by Mel's little brother. Would knowing more about birth control and Plan B have helped or hurt Kara? Do you think middle and high school students should have access to information about birth control, reproductive health and sexuality through their schools? Why or why not?

How well do you think Kara's parents handled finding out that she was pregnant? Were you surprised by the way her parents reacted to her upsetting news? In what ways does Kara's relationship with her parents change during the course of the novel? Discuss scenes in the book where these changes happen.

Near the novel's end, Kara runs into Emma on her way to school. Emma asks what it's like to be in high school. Kara talks about taking responsibility for her actions, and Emma says, "You sound like our life skills teacher." Kara thinks that Emma will have to find out "the truth of things" for herself. Can we learn from others' experiences, from books, or from the media and then apply our own feelings and thoughts to a situation, or does everyone have to learn "the hard way"? Find examples both in the novel and in your own life to support your answer.

Kara's mother and father were raised with certain beliefs about reproductive rights and euthanasia—issues concerning when life begins and ends. When they find out that their daughter is pregnant, Kara's parents are forced to consider the idea of abortion from a more personal and direct perspective. How do you think Kara's becoming pregnant affected her parents' beliefs, and why?

Which comes first—our beliefs, or the way that we think about and judge the circumstances and people in our lives? Are Kara's beliefs about women's reproductive rights in the novel something that she's learned from her parents, or her religion, or both? Does Kara learn to think for herself by the end of the novel? Give some evidence from the story to support your opinion.

If the Supreme Court overturned *Roe v. Wade*, how do you think it would affect women's rights to make their own reproductive choices? How do you think it would affect everyday life in America?

Resources

WEBSITES / BLOGS:

Mariska.com

Mariska Hargitay's (of *Law & Order: SVU*) Web site and blog for teens. (See joyfulheartfoundation.org, below.)

Sexetc.org

This site provides sex ed for teens, by teens, as well as confidential access to adult experts to answer your questions about teen sexual health.

Teensource.org

Get information on sexual health, relationships, and issues that affect teens today. Find answers to your questions, and get helpful advice for making good choices in your life.

Teenwire.com

Planned Parenthood's Web site for teens.

HELPFUL ORGANIZATIONS:

Backupyourbirthcontrol.org or call 1-888-not-2-late

Learn more about emergency contraception and where you can find it in your area.

Catholicsforchoice.org or call 1-202-986-6093

Catholics for Choice (CFC) was founded in 1973 to serve as a voice for Catholics who believe that the Catholic tradition supports a woman's moral and legal right to follow her conscience in matters of sexuality and reproductive health.

Guttmacher.org

The Guttmacher Institute offers a social science research perspective on sexual and reproductive health. A wide range of resources on many topics is provided on this site.

Joyfulheartfoundation.org

The Joyful Heart Foundation was founded by Mariska Hargitay of *Law & Order: SVU*. JHF's mission is to heal, educate, and empower survivors of sexual assault, domestic violence, and child abuse.

Now.org

The National Organization for Women has been supporting women's equality since 1966. Some top priorities: women's reproductive rights, ending gender discrimination and stopping violence against women.

Plannedparenthood.org

Planned Parenthood has health centers which provide reproductive health services and information in every state. You can also call 1-800-230-PLAN to locate a Planned Parenthood near you.

Rainn.org

RAINN is one of the nation's largest anti-sexual assault organizations. Search its crisis center listing page or call 1-800-656-HOPE.

Contact the Author

Thank you for reading *Choices*.

I hope this story of one girl's very personal journey will cause readers to think twice before judging other people's choices from the outside.

Remember: Your life, your choices!

I'd love to hear from you. Please contact me through my website: katebuckleybooks.com